THE IRISH GAME

A NOVEL

THE IRISH GAME

*   *   *

*

J. R. LOWELL

*

*

PRENTICE-HALL, INC. *Englewood Cliffs, N. J.*

The Irish Game by J. R. Lowell

Library of Congress Catalog Card Number: 67–19948

Printed in the United States of America

T50617

Prentice-Hall International, Inc., London
Prentice-Hall of Australia, Pty. Ltd., Sydney
Prentice-Hall of Canada, Ltd., Toronto
Prentice-Hall of India Private Ltd., New Delhi
Prentice-Hall of Japan, Inc., Tokyo

To
JODI
for
discovering
the "game,"
and to
STANLEY
for
his faith,
this book
is dedicated

FOREWORD

This is a story based on the truth, but with some liberties freely taken. If it should seem somewhat wild and unbelievable, in Ireland truth does have a strange way of resembling fiction, and make-believe has a habit of coming true. This story is enmeshed in both truth and make-believe, and where one begins and the other leaves off is of little consequence. If it didn't happen exactly as told herein, it most certainly could have, and if it could have then perhaps it did. There are those who say it did, and others who say it didn't. Some who even claim to have taken part in it. Research never quite established which of these groups was telling the truth, since proof and facts exist side by side with denials and fiction. But then this is Ireland, and part of the Irish Game.

THE IRISH GAME

"A kind of exuberant capering 'round a discovered truth"
G. K. Chesterton

PROLOGUE

It was 1939, a few minutes before eight P.M., two days before Christmas. Dubliners were crowding the streets preparing for the holiday.

At the Phoenix Park ammunition depot—or Magazine Fort as it was called—thirteen men wearing the drab-toned uniforms of the Irish Regular Army settled down for a long night of guard duty.

At the same time on the opposite end of the city, thirty-six men got into twelve trucks and drove toward Phoenix Park. Thirty-six men. Butchers, barbers, postmen, bartenders. Lawyers, doctors, teachers and shopkeepers. Husbands, fathers, brothers and sons. Young and not so young. Thirty-six members of the outlawed Irish Republican Army, the famous, and to some, infamous IRA. Huddled together in threes, tension was a live thing within each cab as the trucks sped through the night.

At eight-thirty, the bell at the outer gate of the Fort rang loudly. The sentry walked through the inner gate—and neglected to close it. Nor did he notify the officer in charge that someone was at the gate.

He peered through the tiny grilled window. There was a heavily-mufflered figure carrying a bulky parcel, supposedly for the officer in charge. The parcel was too big to fit through the window, so the sentry opened the outer gate. He found himself staring into the long thin barrel of a revolver. Without a word he raised his hands above his head.

Within a minute, men were inside the Fort, trucks inside the gates. By ten-thirty all of the Magazine Fort's stock was inside the trucks. Over a million rounds of rifle and machine-gun ammunition. There hadn't been a harsh word spoken, nor a drop of blood shed.

As Dublin prepared for sleep, the thirty-six men sped away to hide their bounty.

✳

A fat man known as Charley paced the floors of a small farmhouse outside of Dublin's city limits. He knew the men were due back. For he had master-minded the raid down to the last detail.

The sound of an automobile. Footsteps. And three men entered. All had gone according to plan. The merchandise was at that moment being stowed away.

Charley was pleased. One of the men though, hung back, disturbed.

"I was wonderin'," he began, "why we had to stow the ammunition all over the bleedin' countryside, instead of hidin' it along with the guns."

Silence. Three pairs of eyes stared at Charley as the blood drained from his face.

"The what?" he asked.

"The guns, man. The guns. You're not expectin' us to *spit* all those lovely bullets at the British, are ye?"

"You've got the guns, haven't ye Charley?" another man asked.

Charley trembled, but like the military genius he was, he pulled himself together. His voice thundered out:

"WELL YE CANNOT BE EXPECTIN' A MAN TO THINK OF EVERYTHING, CAN YE?"

CHAPTER ONE

A WINTRY COLD wind blowing off the River Liffey greeted Chris Kinsella. The weather matched his mood, as he took long strides down rain-splattered O'Connell Street.

As he crossed the avenue toward his tram stop, he gazed with interest at the girls showing a bit more of their legs than they would on a less windy day. The cold wind that whistled through the streets had some good points, he mused. For the first time that day his spirits rose.

Chris was a ruggedly handsome man, who usually took

life's ups and downs with aplomb. Except on cold rainy days and on days when he had to go to tea at his future mother-in-law's home. And on this day after Christmas the Fates had conspired against him. He was expected at the home of Bridie O'Meara, mother of his adored Caitlin.

He scowled, and drew his head down deep into his coat. But blast it all, duty was duty, he reflected darkly as he trudged down O'Connell Street with its cinemas and shops, restaurants and bookstores. Past Lord Nelson gazing imperiously from his towering pillar. Past the General Post Office where almost twenty-four years before a fine group of Irishmen had barricaded themselves against the Black and Tans and gotten slaughtered in the struggle for freedom. Chris felt that he was about to meet a similar end as he headed for the home of one of those martyrs to swill the unfortified tea of his widow.

He waited at his tram stop like a man en route to the guillotine. When the double-deckered tumbril came, he got in and sank into a seat. He glanced at his fellow passengers, but all he saw were newspapers. Newspapers screaming out the story of the Phoenix Park raid. Still no capture of the culprits. Still no recovery of the stolen ammunition. Chris's gloom deepened. Not because of political convictions, but because he knew the reaction of the O'Meara household. Bridie was still fighting for her treacherously-partitioned country. A victory like this would not go uncelebrated.

Life in Dublin was becoming dour indeed. There was no ordinary conversation anymore, only arguments. Chris longed for the times when a man could talk to his chums all evening, without ever coming to any conclusions. With the war in Europe, joyful discussion was becoming a lost art in Ireland, especially at the O'Meara home. If she thinks she's goin' to force me into agreein' with her—or disagreein'—she's daft indeed, he thought.

To get away from his present troubles, Chris let himself drift into his favorite daydream. That of a long-forgotten uncle who had emigrated to America after the Trouble, and naturally made a fortune in that land of gold-paved streets. Then this considerate relative dies—at an old age, of course—and thoughtfully leaves all his money to his only nephew. Then Chris marries lovely, long-legged Caitlin, buys a huge house in the country with a pair of vicious wolfhounds trained to attack his mother-in-law on sight. But he had no uncle in America. No Kinsella could ever manage to lay one pound alongside another, much less have the money for a ticket to that Promised Land.

Blast it, he cursed, it's a drink I need and it's a drink I'm going to have. He stumbled off the tram just as it was starting up. I'd best not, he told himself, Caitlin would have me head. But then a trap disguised as a pub blocked his way. He might as well fortify himself. He downed a pair of double Jameson's, popped a fistful of cloves into his mouth, and continued on.

✳

Chris was met at the door by Bridie O'Meara's glare of disapproval. She sailed past him on to the kitchen—to reheat the water that had cooled because he was late. He sank into a loveseat and faced Beryl, his future sister-in-law. He knew her patriotic mind only too well, and with what disdain she viewed his indifference to the Organization. And how she begrudged him his freedom while her fiancé Liam languished away in Mountjoy Prison.

17

His eyes met Caitlin's. He winked assuringly at her as he noticed the newspaper on the tea trolley. The headlines reminded him of what was to come. If only he had the courage to say a few words about thievery from one's own government.

An ample hip against the kitchen door and Bridie was back with the tea. Cups clattered as Bridie filled them, passed them to Beryl who in turn handed them out.

"And how are ye feelin' this day, Mrs. O'Meara?" I'll be double-damned if I'll ever call her Mum, he added silently.

"I'm fine and dandy, Christopher Kinsella, thank you. Fine and dandy for the first time in ages. And I'm feeling this way because me poor betrayed country is on its way to bein' liberated and whole once more. D'ye see?" she added, just in case he didn't.

Chris knew her question called for no answer, so he offered none.

"Are you ill, Chistopher?" she asked, with disarming solicitude.

What devilish trap was she leading him into? "Ill? No."

"Then you've been drinking. You've been suckin' cloves and don't you be denyin' it. When a body sucks cloves it's either because he's sick to his stomach or he's been drinkin'. And since you've admitted to not bein' ill. . . ."

Chris sighed heavily.

"And don't be sighin' at me like a sick cow. If it's bored ye are sittin' in me house, if ye find it too Irish for your Anglo-Saxon tastes, there's no one compellin' ye to stay. Ye'll not be the first man I've asked to leave, even if it does mean breakin' me poor Caitlin's heart." She turned to her eldest daughter. "Those other two weren't good enough for you, Luv. Neither is this one. Warmin' his backside whilst brave lads half his age are out doin' men's work makin' Ireland free."

"She's talking about the raid on the Magazine Fort," Beryl added.

"Right," Bridie continued. "Allow me to be tellin' you somethin' Christopher. I met me Clancy when he was hidin' out in me own father's house, and we were married in the basement. He loved me, but the Organization always came first. And after a bit it came first with me too. It still does. Me father is long dead, and so is Clancy, but the Organization lives. There's not a thing that's more important than the dream of a land undivided among Irishmen. So when I read of thirty-six fine young men endangerin' their lives outsmartin' the Regular Army, me heart swells with the pride of it."

"When I see you here so safe and snug, it makes me sick. Mind, it's not that I've anything personal against you, but it seems to me that if you cannot find it in yourself to take part in these glorious doin's, then the least you can do is rejoice like the rest of us." Her finger stabbed the air. "For I'm tellin' you that this raid is of a very portentous nature."

Chris stirred, catching Caitlin's glance. She's warnin' me to hold me tongue. She fears there's going to be trouble. Caitlin, me love, I've a terrible feelin' that if she doesn't quit now there will be.

"It's true," Beryl said. "Everything Mum has said is the Lord's truth. It's a pity you can't see it. It's sorry we all are that you don't join a movement that can make good use of you."

Chris drew in his breath. "It's sorry I am that you're sorry, but it's a fight I cannot consider worthy of gettin' involved in."

He wished he'd swallowed those words. Yet in a way

he was glad he hadn't. How many afternoons had they gone over the same thing, facing each other like stray cats? It was time something else was said.

Then Bridie leaned forward in her chair and almost jabbed Chris with her finger.

"You don't realize the portentous nature of this raid," she said. "There's no tellin' what our brave lads might be plannin' to do with all that grand ammunition."

Saints preserve us, she's off and runnin', Chris thought. 'Tis the day after Christmas and there's a world beyond these walls where people are leapin' and playin' and makin' love, and here I am trapped with this man-eatin' dinosaur.

The dinosaur looked at him. "Say something, man. Are ye dead, or what? What kind of Irishman are ye that has not a word on yer tongue, an opinion in yer brain, or a fight in yer fist? Speak up. Ye cannot be denyin' the importance of what's been happenin', now can ye?"

What the hell does she want of me? "I cannot deny the importance of it . . . to some people." What had made him add those three words?

"What the hell d'ye mean . . . to some people?" Bridie tore into him. "To ALL people, I'm tellin' ye." She whirled upon her eldest daughter. "And you," she shouted as the storm gathered strength. "If you'd spend more of your time gettin' involved in your country's doin's instead of showin' your legs at the Gaiety dancin' for a bunch of gapin' fools, perhaps the type of boyfriend you'd have would be different than this one."

Bridie returned to her seat. Without a pause Beryl picked up the gauntlet. Batten down the hatches, Chris thought grimly, a new storm's full upon us. No one was more hysterical than young Beryl, a martyr because of her Liam. Poor lout, if he knew what's good for him he'd

20

stay put. A fine nurse she is. Makin' bombs to blow up people instead of helpin' them. She's a maniac she is, and so's that mother of hers.

Should he tell them all off, and be damned to the consequences? Why the hell not? God's merciful teeth, was he a man or wasn't he?

Chris found himself on his feet. He looked down at the three O'Meara women. Bridie, eyes narrowed dangerously; Beryl, mouth open in surprise, and Caitlin flashing a look of warning.

—"If you people insist on playin' intrigue, raidin' government property, fosterin' a revolution not wanted by the majority, and constructin' bleedin' bombs to be placed in mailboxes to injure innocent people whose only crime is wantin' to post a letter, then you all deserve to be locked up in Mountjoy."

He was in command. He'd stood up on his two feet in this house for the first time. Odd, what happens to a man when he stands up on his own two feet. Then Bridie advanced on him, bringing her purple-flushed face and hot breath up close.

"Don't you be lecturin' me," she hissed. "You don't know how it was, and you've no interest in how it should be. So don't be lecturin' me."

"I know as much about how it was as you do. There's nothing finer in our history than the Easter Rebellion of '16. But we agreed to partition, and that's the end of it. What the hell are you tryin' to do? Start a bloody civil war?"

"It's certain I am that you've been drinkin'. The devil is in you today for sure."

"Stop it," Caitlin broke in. "I'm sick of all this wrangling. Why don't you leave him alone, Mum? Why must you always be managing people's lives for them?"

21

Bridie turned to her eldest daughter. Her mouth opened, then closed. Her voice was calm. "Caitlin O'Meara, don't you ever speak to me like that again. I'll not have it, d'ye hear? Now sit down and behave with the respect a daughter gives a mother in a Christian house."

"And you, get out of my house. Out of my house and away from my daughter. You're a traitor to Holy Ireland."

It was too late to stop. He must keep going. "How in hell can I be a traitor to a cause long dead? You and your Organization. Livin' in the past. Makin' cripples of people is all you're accomplishin'. You won't be satisfied until you have your two daughters thrown into Mountjoy."

"You're a coward, Christopher Kinsella. Afraid to take sides. Afraid to get yourself an honest job so you can marry the girl who's been wastin' her youth and beauty waitin' for you. It's glad I am that your poor parents are dead or they'd die of shame I'm certain. Now ye'll be gettin' your worthless carcass out of me house. Out, until you're ready to apologize for insultin' a defenseless woman."

The defenseless woman grabbed Chris's shirt front, got hold of his belt, and pulled him to the door. Out the front door, down the stone steps. His hat and coat followed.

Chris mumbled as he sat in a puddle, "No way to treat a man. No way at all, especially a man who but a moment ago was standin' on his own two feet."

His head spun. Wet and stunned, he got to his feet. His shame hurt more than his bruises. And Caitlin had witnessed his shame. Had seen him tossed out of her house like a sack of garbage. A man who so recently and firmly had stood upon his two feet.

He had to think. Something to even the score, settle

the books, balance the scales. He faced the O'Meara house, source of his shame, and a shout of protest rose from within him, echoing in the still air.

"Holy Ireland me arse!"

CHAPTER TWO

FURY ACCOMPANIED CHRIS through Dublin's rain-drenched streets, and propelled him to the house of Peadar Dougherty. Peadar was the one person he could turn to.

"Tis a proper crumbled sight you are," his friend greeted him. "And what you're needing is a drop of some hard stuff, right?"

Chris sank into an armchair. Peadar could guess what had happened to his friend. The afternoon sessions at the O'Meara household usually ended this way.

"Called me a traitor she did," Chris said. "In front of Caitlin too. A coward and a traitor. Her very words."

"And what did you do?"

"What'd I do?" Chris bellowed. "I'll tell ye what I did. I stood up on me own two feet for once, that's what I did."

"Bully for you, lad. And what did she do when you did?"

Chris's pride faded, as he told Peadar what happened. "But I'm not beaten yet. Not by a long shot. There's a grand plan rushin' about in me brain. A plan that'll take care of the lot of 'em.

"You well know, Peadar lad, that I'm not usually angry or vindictive. Violence is foreign to me nature. It's more reflective I am. Well, I've been reflectin.' And I have a wondrous plan for gettin' me revenge." He paused.

"Let's hear your wondrous plan," Peadar said.

"It's spinnin' a web I am. A lovely and entanglin' web." His voice dropped to a conspiratorial whisper as he told Peadar his idea for getting even with Bridie O'Meara, and for striking a blow against the whole crew of conspirators. He outlined his points. Bridie's contact with the IRA was one Denis Duffy, an insignificant little mouse, who acted as if he alone were responsible for the Phoenix Park raid. Duffy was a crony of Seamus Murphy, minor IRA official and owner of a dockside pub. Murphy had underground contacts with foreign sailors who came in and out of port. Before the war, they smuggled such harmless contraband articles as contraceptives and books published in France. Their pre-war sideline grew into the gathering and transmitting of more or less inconsequential information to the German Legation in Lisbon. They felt they were doing their patriotic part in harassing the

British enemy, in return for Germany's promise to help in the struggle for Irish reunification.

"And that's me plan," Chris concluded. "To give those busy little bees a chance to do some real spyin'. I intend to post some vital information to Bridie with a note signed Fellow Patriot. She'll take it directly to Duffy. He'll take it to Murphy. And Murphy will get it to the Germans in Lisbon through his sea-goin' pals. And they'll get it to German Intelligence in Berlin."

"And then all hell breaks loose. Because when the Germans get the 'vital' information our friends will find that their days of rushin' about actin' important have ended. Don't ye see?"

"What I see," Peadar said, "is that your plan will make heroes out of the very ones you're aimin' to destroy."

"Not quite true! The vital information I'll be sendin' won't be so very vital. Now on your feet, lad. We've a hard night's work ahead of us manufacturin' it."

✳

At Tenth Army Headquarters building in Hamburg, Germany, Colonel Siegfried von Falkenhorst, Abwehr II Army Intelligence, sat at his desk. He had been there for a week, ever since he had heard of the raid on the Dublin Magazine Fort. He had big plans. Colonel von Falkenhorst came from a long line of soldiers. But unlike his forebears he wasn't satisfied with being a soldier. He wanted to be a general. This was the purpose of the years of assiduous plotting that got him where he was.

He glanced at his watch. Any moment the man who was to be the instrument for his future success would enter his office. His stomach muscles contracted, and he reached for a black market Alka-Seltzer tablet. It annoyed him that a man such as he had no control over his stomach. It disturbed him even more than his quiescent syphilis. At least that was a man's disease, to be borne with pride, especially since the rumors about Der Fuehrer had reached his ears.

The inter-office buzzer sounded, and a most undistinguished-looking man in his forties of medium height and build entered. Hans Ernst Pflug.

This was the man von Falkenhorst had been training for the secret Irish task. This was the man who was the only Irish expert in all the Fatherland. Exactly the man von Falkenhorst needed to help him become a general.

He had explained to Pflug how all the inefficient cloak-and-dagger men sent to Ireland by the SS in the past had been picked up within twenty-four hours. Those men were spies. They knew all about spying, but nothing about the Irish. Von Falkenhorst knew that the Irish needed a man who knew Ireland. A man who could help Germany make use of the discontented groups in Ireland to harass the British. But the SS felt that the Irish were too irresponsible.

Von Falkenhorst gave Pflug a copy of the *London Times*. It was the issue announcing the raid on the Magazine Fort. "Was that the work of irresponsible people? Of course not. The SS have no imagination. They only know how to send in their spies—not how to organize people. This action on the Magazine Fort has convinced me that I was right all along about these people. And look at these maps that just came from our man Duffy in Dublin."

Under the astonished gaze of Lieutenant Pflug was a collection of finely drawn maps of Ireland indicating port facilities, military installations, ammunition depots, railway heads, coves suitable for U-boat refueling stations and remote points for secret radio and weather reporting stations.

"These are important," said von Falkenhorst. "We must take advantage of them."

It would be Lieutenant Pflug's job to parachute into Ireland and coordinate the forces. He was to help form a strong German-Irish alliance. Instill a bit of German know-how into their activities. Prepare them for the eventual dropping of paratroops.

One thing the Colonel didn't tell Pflug was that the mission was so secret that only the two of them would know about it until—and unless—it succeeded. Nobody in official Berlin would know of him. He would not be mentioned in the War Diary. If he failed, no one would know.

"I'm putting through a captaincy for you," von Falkenhorst said. "That and your instructions will be waiting for you at your point of departure. Now take a few days leave, and get your affairs in order. And Captain Pflug, should you get into any trouble in Ireland you will be on your own. Is that clear?"

"Am I to be supplied with a vial of poison, sir?"

"You've seen too many movies, my dear Captain. If I wanted a cloak-and-dagger man I would've gotten one. You are a liaison agent. Liaison agents do not take poison. You will not get caught. Is that understood?"

"Yes sir."

Von Falkenhorst's manner softened. "Who knows what this day is going to lead to, my dear Pflug. For both of us," he added as he pictured himself in his general's uniform.

He told Pflug to await further orders at his home in Munden.

Master Plan "Danny Boy" was in its final phase.

*

*

CHAPTER THREE

*

HANS ERNST PFLUG had been born too late. Had he weighed less and arrived earlier, his mother might have remained earthbound long enough to have influenced him with her gentle spirit. As it was, she lived just long enough to hear the doctor announce that it was a boy, and to swiftly decide that with two male Pflugs to contend with, it would be a losing fight. So with a sigh, she relinquished the chance to regenerate the Pflug line, and died.

From this mournful beginning came the man who was to become Germany's master spy. His father bade his wife good-bye and delivered his son into the capable arms of Anna, housekeeper for two generations of Pflugs. "See that he always sleeps in a cool room," said senior Pflug.

Hans Ernst Pflug had not only been born late, but as far as anyone could tell, humorless. And with his father as an example, that's the way he continued to grow. To Anna, no Pflug could do wrong. To his father, everything he did was right because he obeyed his orders. By the time he was fourteen he was a junior edition of the senior Pflug. He was a thin, almost ascetic-looking boy with serious brown eyes looking out from a worried face. He had the open innocence of his mother and the closed mind of his father. But there was something of his own too—a scholarly brilliance that even his father couldn't cope with alone. So Hans was turned over to a long line of tutors.

One of these tutors left Hans with a desire to find out all there was to know about a seemingly mythical land called Ireland.

He continued his studies of that strange Celtic country and its people until he was nineteen. They were interrupted by the First World War. His father reminded Hans about his country's glorious past and still more glorious future. The opportunity had come for all true-blooded Germans to defend the Fatherland. The senior Pflug enlisted, taking his reluctant true-blooded son along.

Four years later they returned home. Hans had joined the service as a private. And came out of it a private without even a wound to compensate. Senior Pflug returned as a major—and had a game left leg as well.

Their little town of Munden had not changed. And their mausoleum of a home had been kept spotless by the aging but ageless Anna who was at the door to greet them.

On his first day home Hans went to his room, turned the photograph of von Hindenburg to the wall, put away his uniform and opened his books.

The years passed and Hans's library grew as he collected all the books he could on Ireland. Early Irish history, Christianity in Celtic lands, Irish tradition, and the lives and legends of both St. Patrick and St. Columba. His books ranged from the architecture of Ireland to the antiquities of its countryside. He studied English until he was accent-less. But he never could master Gaelic. There was little he didn't know about his adopted land, but his information was second-hand, from books and maps.

So when his father agreed to raise his allowance, Hans set out on a three-month walking tour of Ireland.

When he returned home he wrote a small book, and then resumed his studies, quietly considering himself an "Irish Expert." While an expert in one area, he was an innocent in others, for although he was thirty, he had never gone to a dance, never kissed a girl, never swore, and except for his four years in the Army and his trip to Ireland, had never left Munden. The years passed uneventfully until 1938, when his father died. By that time Germany was once again preparing for war, and the senior Pflug's final words were, "Your future is with the Army."

Being a dutiful son, Hans again joined the Army. And since he didn't know how to answer the questions they asked him about his profession, hobbies and specific talents, he answered "Irish Expert" for each. The proper authorities were impressed, and this time Hans entered as a lieutenant. A few months later his file was plucked out by Colonel von Falkenhorst.

Thus Hans Ernst Pflug, born too late, had at last made

up for his earlier bad timing by being the right person for
the right job at the right time.

✳

It was the night before his departure. Hans was study-
ing his image in the mirror. Rather a sad-looking agent, he
decided. But then it's better to be a spy who doesn't look
like one than to be a spy who does. A spy who looks like
a spy would no doubt get caught. He felt reassured.

He poured a small glass of sherry, and got out of his
new uniform. He put on his father's woolen bathrobe and
sat down facing the blazing fire. New emotions had been
flooding him since he'd seen von Falkenhorst. Too many
and too new for him to cope with all at once. Excitement,
anticipation, fear. But most of all, there was an overriding
feeling of importance. He was an important man. He
could prove it, to himself, to his father's ghost, to Anna.

In the midst of these thoughts Anna came into his room.
She was wearing a black wool robe that looked as old as
she did. She peered at Hans from behind her old
lorgnette.

"Where's your father's picture? It's not where it should
be."

Hans smiled. Nothing ever escaped Anna. "It's all right,
Anna. I took it down. I'm taking it with me."

"And where are you going this time?"

"To Ireland, Anna. I thought I told you that I'm being
sent there." He saw no harm in confiding in Anna. She
seldom left the house, and spoke to no one when she did.

"So you did, so you did. And why are you leaving so
soon when only two days ago you were in Nuremberg?"

Hans looked affectionately at this gnome-like relic from
his childhood. The old woman had known his father as a

child, and his grandfather as well. She was his only link with the past, the only person left who cared.

"I wasn't in Nuremberg, I was in Hamburg."

"What's the difference? Hamburg, Nuremberg; they're all alike, those big cities. You'd be much better off if you'd stay here in Munden and not go tramping all over the countryside. And why, may I ask, are you taking your father's picture to Hamburg?"

"I'm taking it with me to Ireland," he said.

"To Ireland?" she echoed incredulously. "And why, may I ask, is von Hindenburg sending you there of all places?"

"Not von Hindenberg, Anna. He's gone now, remember?"

"Of course I remember. I may get a bit confused with all your important comings and goings, but all you have to do is remind me, and everything's clear. So why is von Hindenburg sending you off to Ireland?"

Hans's heart sank. She was getting old. He told her again of his mission.

"I'm proud of you, Werner," she murmured when he finshed.

"I'm Hans," he corrected her gently.

"Of course you are. And you should be proud too. But you know I never did approve of your walking trips in foreign lands. Lands peopled with alcoholic devils and with sanitary conditions not up to the standard of the Fatherland's. Why don't you walk through Germany instead?"

"Don't worry about me, Anna. You'll be proud of me when I return."

The old lady nodded sleepily. It was time for Hans to go to bed too.

His dreams were of his mission. Of success. Of his return to Germany. He was climbing out of the submarine that had been sent to pick him up. There on the dock was Colonel von Falkenhorst. Saluting smartly, Hans reports mission accomplished and ready for new assignment. Von Falkenhorst leads him to a large limousine. They're driven to Berlin where there is a reception in his honor. He's seated between Der Fuehrer and Goering. From across the table, Himmler himself promotes Hans to full colonel in charge of Intelligence. They drink champagne from conquered France. And pretty girls come to dance with him.

His eyes snapped open. No! No girls. This was no time for such weakness. He sighed. Such splendid dreams. Dreams that could actually come to pass.

Destiny had called, and Hans was ready.

CHAPTER FOUR

✳

BEHIND A STACK of potato pancakes sat Herr Doctor Franz Martin Poetsch, German Ambassador to Dublin. He cut the pancakes into triangles and stuffed them into his mouth. His eyes never left the plate. His wife sat across from him, trying to determine from his expression whether or not her pancakes were a success.

As he chewed, he thought of Hulda Grutze, the woman who made the pancakes. His wife. Why had he married this woman taller than he, who measured the success of her marriage by the growth of her mate's waistline? Was it because of the potato pancakes, or her father, an influential government official? Whatever the true reason, he had long ago forgotten it. Though it was her father who was responsible for the good life he was now leading. He was careful to keep his eyes from his daughter Lore. Dr. Poetsch couldn't stand her any more than he could her mother.

He liked being in this neutral capital. He had time to read, to listen to good music, to eat well. Nothing like a post in a neutral country during a war.

At first, he had problems with Army Intelligence. They wanted him to play their spy games. They even installed —over his objections—a secret wireless. But he'd have no part of it, and continued sending his messages through the normal cable system via Switzerland. Finally, he convinced them it was all a waste of time. He was especially glad to learn of the finale to the story of the recent raid. Exactly what one could expect from the Irish. But it was a stroke of genius for them to sell part of the stolen ammunition back to the Army.

His thoughts were interrupted by a soft knock on the door, followed by the eager young face of Volker Scherrf.

"What is it, Scherrf?" Dr. Poetsch demanded of his attaché.

Scherrf inched a bit more of himself into the room trying to avoid the eager eyes of Lore. Volker Scherrf was the only male in the Legation near her age.

"I beg your pardon, Herr Ambassador. But an imporant message just came in on the wireless."

The Ambassador sighed. "Well, what does it say? Read it to me. My wife and daughter aren't spies, you know."

Scherrf came into the room completely. He walked sideways like a crab to keep away from Lore. He hadn't anything against her personally; he just didn't like women in general.

"Top Secret. Message 218. Hamburg. Special Agent arriving Dublin within week. Mission most important. Give all possible assistance if contacted. Inform our man in IRA, Denis Duffy, of arrival and importance of strictest secrecy. Password is Danny Boy. End of message."

"Damn it," exploded Dr. Poetsch. This was too much. He had been assured that things like this wouldn't happen to him anymore. And now after a few months of peace this had to arrive. "Who signed that message?"

"A Colonel von Falkenhorst."

Dr. Poetsch ordered a message to go out at once to this interfering von Falkenhorst informing him in no uncertain terms that since Berlin had ordered hands off Ireland, the German Legation in that country was not to be used to play ridiculous little games of espionage. "And don't send it over his goddamned wireless," he added. "Let it go by pouch through our Swiss Legation."

Scherrf looked up from his notes. "Shall I inform this man Duffy, or . . . ?"

"Yes, inform him. Inform him to see that his 'special agent' stays far away from me!"

Frau Poetsch looked worried. "Now, now, Putzi, remember your nerves." She placed a fat moist hand on his. He shrank back, not so much from the hand as from the hated nickname.

"I'm going to my study," he announced. "Bring me a couple of bottles of beer."

"But too much beer isn't good for your liver, Putzi."

＊

Two men were sipping coffee at the office of The Red House in Park Gate, Dublin.

The telephone rang, one of the men answered, turned

to the other, "It's the constable up at Sligo. An RAF plane coming in from sea patrol made a forced landing there. He wants instructions."

Herbert Gallagher took the phone. "Inspector Gallagher here. Feed the poor lads, Constable, and send them on their way. Give them a bit of butter and a steak or two to take back with them, and fill their tanks with petrol. And Constable . . . don't forget to get a receipt for the petrol."

"I know what you're thinking, Sean," he said to the other man. "It's necessary for Ireland to be neutral. But it's just a question of whose side we're neutral on."

"I know." Sean Higgens said. "And while we're talking about neutrality, a request came in from the Japanese Legation for permission for a short wave wireless. Sender and receiver. What do we do about it?"

"Grant their request, of course. And arrange for a team of men to monitor it."

It had been an unusually quiet day at headquarters. The old year had ended with the raid on the Magazine Fort. Yesterday the last of the stolen ammunition had been recovered. And today all was quiet. And dull. For the raid and the hectic weeks that followed it were not just police work, but a game. With the old game over, Gallagher was especially glad when a police officer came to tell him that a message to the German Legation had just been intercepted.

"Things are looking up already. I wonder what's brought this on. Do you think it was Duffy's maps?" They looked authentic enough, he thought. It was good thinking on the part of that sailor who showed them to the British before delivering them.

"Well, as long as they're informing their man in the IRA, I suppose we ought to inform ours."

"I imagine we should alert some of the boys along the

40

coast to be on the lookout for the new arrival." Higgens added.

"What on earth for? We've no idea where he'll land or when. Why should our lads hang about the countryside in this weather waiting for him? He'll head for Murphy's Pub anyway. Let him find his own way to Dublin."

Once again, the phone. This time it was British Intelligence calling to say a message from Germany had just been monitored in London. Gallagher asked how long ago the message had been received.

"About fifteen minutes ago. We had to decode it."

"And it took you fifteen minutes? We did it in ten."

CHAPTER FIVE

*

PUSHING AND BANGING noises as Bridie sailed about like a battleship. Shoving, tugging and thrashing, she demolished the dust. Next stop was the kitchen, where Caitlin huddled by the stove drinking her morning coffee.

In a voice that defied challenge, Bridie announced that she was going to make a stew for dinner. The carrots she chopped felt the anger boiling in her massive breast.

"I'm dreadfully sorry, Mum," Caitlin said.

Bridie whirled around, eyes blazing. "Don't you be usin' that sympathetic tone of voice on me, Caitlin

O'Meara. It's no sympathy I'm needin'. It isn't a funeral, y'know. We'll not take this scandal lyin' down, ye can be sure. But those monumental idiots! Muckin' up a perfectly good operation like that."

Just then the door bell rang, and Caitlin escaped to open it.

Bridie's voice followed her. "If it's another one of those sympathetic commiserators that's been callin' all morning, I'll not be talkin' to them. D'ye understand?"

"I understand," Caitlin shouted.

"What do you understand?" Chris asked her.

Her gaze moved from Chris's eyes to the newspaper sticking out from his coat pocket. "Oh Chris, you're here to taunt and tease Mum."

"Now what makes you think I'd do a rum thing like that?" he said as Caitlin led him into the kitchen.

"Because you're not the sort to let an opportunity like this get by."

"Now Caitlin, luv, you well know that when it comes to facin' up to that dragon, I'm fair fermentin' with fear."

But as soon as he was settled at the kitchen table, he drew blood by his cheerful greeting. Bridie snarled at him, and went back to the stew.

"There's a most interestin' article on the front page, Caitlin. All about those brave Irish lads with fight in their fists, words on their tongues, but not a brain in their skulls, who raided the Magazine Fort and came away with a load of ammunition—and not a single gun."

"Look at him," Bridie commanded. "Struttin' like a peacock. Hopin' I'll be riled by his tauntin' words to put on a poor mouth in front of him. Well, I'll not be supplyin' ye with that pleasure, Mister Kinsella, d'ye see?"

She knew the battle was lost, but she fought on. She needed the words. Words to use as weapons, words to ease her wounded heart or shut the grinning mouth of the man before her. Though her voice was stilled, her spirit blazed from her eyes, and dared her adversary to continue.

Chris accepted the dare. "Would ye be sayin', Caitlin, that this was a deed to stir the hearts of all true Irishmen? A deed of a great portentous nature? I'd say it's a deed to make the heart of true Irishmen stir all right. Stir with laughter."

"Get him out of me house, Caitlin. Get him out before the control that I'm exercisin' starts fadin', and I do somethin' desperate."

When Chris saw her face turn purple with rage, he stood and backed to the door. "I'm goin'. I'm goin'. Meet ye at the barricades, Mum."

And he was gone.

Caitlin put an arm about her mother's shoulders. "Forgive him, Mum, he's a bit mad you know."

"Be off with ye, girl," Bridie retorted. "He wouldn't be an Irishman if he didn't act as he did. But I'll have the last laugh. You'll see."

"I bear news of momentous import," announced a beaming Denis Duffy.

Until this interruption, Bridie had spent the day pacing, muttering and swearing under her breath. And she burnt the stew. Terrible things had befallen her country. More than a patriotic daughter of Ireland should be made to bear. She and her equally-stricken younger daughter ate an undigestible meal together. After dinner, they hid behind their knitting. Duffy had interrupted them.

"News of momentous import to us all," Duffy continued. But he quailed under Bridie's withering look.

"It better be," she warned. "For I've little mind to spend the evenin' listenin' to any more nonsensical and inconsequential excuses ye may be offerin'. Boys doin' the work of men. Never in all me days have I heard of such monumental bumblin'. You men would never think of lettin' a woman in on your plannin', would ye? We're not good enough for that, are we? We're only to be used for the runnin' of messages whilst the bullets are flyin' about our heads. Or the loadin' of ammunition durin' a fight, or the birthin' of the martyrs for ye. But to make use of the brains the good Lord gave us, never. It's a poor Ireland that has to depend on the likes of you men for her freedom."

"For the love of God, woman," Duffy managed. "Simmer down and don't go on about what's past and done with. I've not come here through the dangers that lurk in the night to rehash the blasted raid. Now calm yourself and listen whilst I inform ye of some excitin' events about to happen."

Duffy told them of the message from the German Legation, and of the Special Agent who was coming. He spoke in a low voice because he imagined danger lurked outside every window. He spoke of all the exciting things the agent would help them accomplish.

Mother and daughter listened until he finished.

"And what'll it be, Denis, me boy? A rebellion of the Six Counties in the north against the Saxon Oppressor, or all of Ireland risin' up together?"

"Now, that's a question that cannot be answered yet. There'll have to be lots of meetin's and top echelon plannin' to be done first."

Exactly what Bridie wanted to hear. She knew that

she'd be part of these goings-on. It all happened because she had the good sense to pass those anonymous maps on to Duffy. After a few tugs on the curly black hairs that sprouted from her chin, she took a bottle of Irish whiskey from the cupboard.

"A toast," she cried. "A toast to Ireland soon to be united."

"And," Duffy broke in, "It's been decided at an emergency meeting of the Organization that the Special Agent is to be hidden out here at the home of Bridie O'Meara."

Bridie rose to the occasion. "We'll have to get the secret room ready. Beryl, bolt the front door and draw the blinds. And play the radio as loud as you can so's no one will overhear us."

She turned to Duffy. "Ye cannot be too cautious in matters such as this."

"That's right." He too was well-versed in this sort of thing.

"Now roll back the rug," Bridie commanded. Her daughter dropped to her knees, and then realized someone would have to move the couch first.

"Denis," Bridie said, "I know 'tis a shame to make a man with brains such as yours use his muscles, but when Ireland's future is at stake we must all make sacrifices. So kindly raise your backside from off that chair, and put your shoulder to the task at hand."

Her command was not to be disobeyed. And soon the trapdoor hidden under the rug was revealed. Bridie herself lifted the creaking lid, and the three of them stared into the blackness of the pit below.

"Make a note," Bridie snapped. "Supplies needed. One —oilcan for trapdoor. Two—stopwatch for practicin' rapid getaways. Three—supplies for the Agent. Stuff like food and books."

"Now to investigate," said Bridie. "Considerin' the sad fact of me waistline and the narrowness of the openin', I hereby delegate you, Denis Duffy, to accomplish that mission. There's a light down there that you should . . ." She was stopped in mid-sentence by the sound of footsteps outside approaching the front door. Quickly the trapdoor was shut, the rug rolled back, the furniture replaced.

The knock on the door turned to pounding as Bridie slid back the bolts.

"What's the idea of bolting the door like that, Mum?" said Caitlin as she looked with amusement at a flushed and puffing Denis Duffy, and a disheveled Beryl. She caught the panic in the three pairs of eyes pinned on her.

"Oh no," she laughed. "Don't tell me he's going to stay *here!*"

"Who?" Bridie asked.

"The spy, of course!" She looked into their shocked faces. "I don't see why you should be so surprised that I know. Have you ever heard of a secret that remained one for very long in this town? They're taking bets over at Neary's as to how long before he's picked up. Twenty-four hours seems to be the maximum."

CHAPTER SIX

※

IN THE SHADOWY belly of the Heinkel HE-3, Special Agent Hans Ernst Pflug was tossed from side to side as the plane fought its way through the storm. When he'd first begun his special course he had told his instructor that he'd already had parachute training. It would have been too complicated otherwise. He would have had to train. And that was dangerous. Actually, not only had Hans never jumped out of a plane, but he'd never even gotten into one. The thought of going up was terrifying; jumping down even worse. He could accept the obvious—the need to go up and down once. But why go through it

dozens of times? He gave von Falkenhorst the answer he
expected and the problem was solved.

He had the same attitude about questions on his being
an Irish Expert. Indeed he was one. But more in the area
of ancient Ireland, its art and culture. Since his Colonel
hadn't asked any questions, Hans hadn't volunteered anything that could have jeopardized this chance for another
trip to his favorite country.

Now, hugging his trembling knees to his chest, he wondered if he'd done the right thing. Better to think of something else. He opened the sealed orders von Falkenhorst
gave him just before take-off:

1. Keep in mind the main objectives of your mission:
   (a) establish contact with Irish Underground
       Army through our agent, Denis Duffy. He
       can be contacted at a beer hall called Mur-
       phy's.
   (b) set up good working relations with same.
   (c) prevent stolen ammunition from being
       wasted on such things as blowing up mail-
       boxes in England.
   (d) establish effective radio link with Abwehr
       II.
   (e) establish weather stations in remote areas
       (see maps).
   (f) establish refueling bases for U-boats on west
       coast (see maps).
   (g) check ammunition depots (see maps).
2. Do not indulge in any espionage at this time, or
   in any military activities. Orders to come later.
3. Should you get into any trouble, get out of it on
   your own. Under no conditions involve Abwehr II
   if you are captured.
   (a) Do not, under any circumstances, contact

German Ambassador in Dublin. He refuses
to cooperate.
4. Destroy this after memorizing.

Hans re-read number 3. Then he went to 4, and tore the
sheet of paper into tiny bits. He ate them.

Suddenly bursting anti-aircraft shells sounded all about
him. He heard the rapid exchange between the pilot and
the navigator. They had somehow flown over British ter-
ritory. They zoomed upward and to the left. Silence once
more. Hans breathed evenly again.

He reviewed the things he'd brought in his water-
proofed suitcase. A complete set of English tweeds and a
topcoat, both with London labels; a loaf of bread, some
cheese, sausages and a bottle of brandy. A South African
passport in his own name, shaving equipment, toothbrush
and paste, soap and washcloth, comb and brush, hand
mirror and the framed photograph of his father. Hidden in
the middle of this collection was a wallet containing 3000
English pounds, and a copy of James Joyce's *Ulysses*
printed in English. This was his code book for making up
messages to von Falkenhorst. Hans couldn't wait to get
started. He pictured a message:

ULSTER SHIPPING FACILITIES DESTROYED. NEXT STOP
LIVERPOOL.   PFLUG.

The voice of the navigator broke in. "We're over your
drop point, Captain."

"So soon? Are you sure?"

"Of course. If you don't want to fly back with us, prepare to drop."

Hans stumbled to his feet, checked the suitcase
strapped to his belt, and picked up his wireless set at-

tached to a parachute of its own. He watched the bomb
bay open slowly.

"Are you sure?" he asked again.

"You better get going, Captain. We can't hang around
here all night."

Hans was sure the man was nervous. He stood by the
yawning pit of blackness at his feet and stared down.

"Heil Hitler," the navigator said as he helped Hans on
his way.

✳

Down he went, eyes tightly shut. The engines of the
plane roared in the distance. When Hans pulled the ring
on his chest, his fall was checked by the opening of the
parachute. He opened his eyes and saw blackness. Where
was he falling? He felt cold. And then he felt as if he were
no longer falling. But that was impossible. No time to
figure it out.

The first thing he had to do was let go of the wireless
set. With a prayer that it wouldn't land too far away from
where he did, he pulled the ring of the second 'chute and
let go.

The sound of the plane had by now faded completely.
He was surrounded by silent blackness. He had to relax,
so he would hit ground with his muscles ready to absorb
the shock. He'd heard somewhere that this was the right
way to land. He hoped he would fall into something soft
like a haystack. This wasn't impossible. He was landing in
the farm country.

He was getting wetter and colder. It was unbearable.
He opened his mouth to protest. And it was filled with the
icy saltiness of the Irish Sea.

CHAPTER SEVEN

DOWN, DOWN HE sank, struggling to free himself from the entangling embrace of his parachute. He slipped out of the harness and gasped and choked his way upward. His job right now was to get to shore. With the sound of waves breaking in the distance, he began his long swim.

After what seemed like hours, he felt the powerful surge of the waves pushing him toward the shore. The sound of their crashing grew louder. He relaxed and let the sea carry him toward safety. He was unprepared for the bone-bruising landing on the rocky beach.

He lay there, unmoving, face down among the rocks, his wet clothes clinging to his aching muscles.

He dragged himself up. The rain was not as heavy now. And at least the problem of staying alive was solved. It was time for Hans to face his other problems. Where was he? How far from his drop point? Where was his wireless? His parachute?

For the first time in his life Hans Pflug was sorry he didn't know enough curse words to adequately express his feelings.

He had to find someplace warm. Had to sleep. But the mission came first. The success of the mission was at stake.

First he had to get into his civilian clothes and bury his uniform. He walked until he came to a grassy knoll. He unhooked the heavy case strapped to his belt, stripped off his soaked clothing, and put on his dry underwear, flannel shirt and British tweed suit and overcoat.

But he had forgotten to pack a change of shoes. Not only did he have to put his feet back into those water-logged army boots, but how incongruous they'd look with his civilian clothes. He shrugged. There was nothing he could do about it. Fully dressed, he dug a grave for his new uniform. He would have to leave the lost wireless and the parachutes to the Fates. He picked up his suitcase and set out.

After about a quarter of a mile, he came to what on a dry day must have been a wagon road. Now it was a muddy obstacle course. But there in the distance was the outline of a house. As he approached it, the door swung open. Hans dropped to the ground, his face in the mud. A good move. For how would he explain why he didn't know where he was or where he came from? Better to wait for daylight before asking for help.

What if he were in Ulster and not Southern Ireland? If so, he shouldn't have buried his uniform. If caught there'd be nothing between him and a firing squad.

He raised his head, and at the door was a man with his nightshirt hanging out of his heavy coat. He was carrying a kerosene lamp.

What should he do? Identify himself in the hopes that the farmer was a sympathizer? Or remain still. The decision was made for him. The beam of light swung over the terrain, and then the farmer went back in the house.

Hans dashed across the field, into the barn. There with the pigs, he fashioned a bed of straw on which to sleep away the bleak winter night.

The farmer was on the phone making his report to the Organization. Surely his duty didn't include getting pneumonia while trying to convince the poor fool to come in out of the cold.

Night passed into morning. A cold and dark morning. Hans stretched his aching muscles, then washed and shaved, using the water from the pig trough. After a hurried breakfast of sausages, bread and brandy, he crept out of the barn.

The dampness of the winter dawn was settling over the countryside. The air smelled of burning peat. The hollows of the gentle hills were pocketed with grey-blue shadows, and in the hush not a bird sang nor creature stirred, human or animal. As Hans crept around the farmhouse, he was brought up short by the smell of percolating coffee and frying bacon. His stomach contracted. But the smell meant the farmer was awake. He had to hurry.

*

As Hans rushed away, the farmer appeared at the door, coffee pot in hand. He opened his mouth to call out, but then changed his mind. He wasn't the sort who'd stop a man as determined-looking as Hans from going about his business. The farmer returned to his kitchen for an extra large breakfast.

*

The sound of the rising wind brought a sense of doom to Hans. This life of danger wasn't for him. He loved Ireland, but why did he have to be in a part of it that he knew nothing about? He should have landed in an area he had walked through years before, the places of antiquity he longed to revisit. But that cowardly navigator had dropped him instead in this bleak and barren place.

He slogged along in his rain-soaked boots. With each step, he grew more furious at the Irish. How inefficient not even to have someone on the lookout for him to guide him into Dublin. But this inefficiency only confirmed their need for him.

*

As Hans walked, curious eyes peered at him through parted curtains. The telephone wires to Dublin were busy, as reports were called in either to the police, or to the Organization.

Hans strode on. After a few hours, he saw that the groupings of farmhouses were growing more frequent, and the dirt road was widening. He must be approaching a town. There was a signpost up ahead. He was dumfounded to see that it was obliterated with black paint. As he stared at it, a boy on a bicycle came toward him. Hans signaled him.

"Could you tell me where I am?"

"Aye," the boy replied.

"Well then would you be so kind to do so?"

"I might. It depends on why you're wantin' to know."

"Because I'm lost, that's why." Hans had forgotten that this was the usual turn conversations seemed to take in this strange country.

"You mean you don't know where you are? How come?"

Hans sighed. He must have been led into this trap. "I'm a South African on a walking trip, and I've lost my way because of the storm. If I knew what town I was near, I could get my bearings and continue on my way."

"And where would that be?"

"Dublin. And since that signpost is blacked out, I can't tell where I am, can I?"

"That's right."

"Well, why is it blacked out?"

"Because they all are. If the Germans decide to invade us they'll not be knowin' where they are." He grinned. "Same as you."

Then the boy informed Hans he was within a mile of a town called Kilmuckridge. Hans asked if there was a railroad station near.

The boy nodded.

"Where?"

"About a mile from here."

"And do you know when the next train leaves for Dublin?"

"Well now that I don't. But I can tell you when the last one left."

"When was that?"

"Fourteen years ago."

The boy mounted his bicycle and rode on. Hans sank to the grass on the side of the road and got out his map of Ireland. At least he saw that Kilmuckridge wasn't in Ulster. It was South of Dublin.

As Hans pored over his map, he began to feel that he was being watched. He looked up. His heart sank. He couldn't get arrested now. He couldn't fail like those SS dolts. It couldn't happen. It mustn't happen.

"Good morning to you," said Constable McCleary.

"Good morning, sir."

The Constable noticed the open case beside Hans. "Now you wouldn't be a commercial traveler would you by any chance?"

"That's right, sir. I'm a commercial traveler on my way up to Dublin."

"Now that's what I'd be calling an accomodating coincidence," Constable McCleary said as he squatted down beside the case. "You wouldn't be in the haberdashery line now would you?"

Hans's mind reeled. What was haberdashery? What should he be carrying if he were in that line? What an odd word. Must be Gaelic. He decided to chance it. "Yes, I am."

"That's a bit of luck that is. I'm needing a little help and you're just the right man. One of my suspender buttons has come off, and I wonder if you'd be so kind as to sell me a safety pin."

The Constable began to rummage through Hans's case. He saw the maps and sketches and the copy of *Ulysses*.

"This is contraband," he informed Hans. He moved the sausages out of the way and saw the wallet crammed with pound notes. He whistled.

"Business must be good." Then he noticed the photograph of the Senior Pflug in full Wehrmacht uniform. "Relative of yours?"

Constable McCleary closed the case and ordered Hans to follow him into town.

"Why?" Hans managed.

"Oh, it's not because you're carrying about on your person a book that's been banned from our shores. It's because you're what we refer to as a suspicious character. Why you might even be one of those German spies that have been falling in on us of late."

"What are you going to do with me?"

"Well now, if you're not one of those spies, there's nothing to worry about. But if you are, there's nothing we can do but hang you."

Hans cursed the luck that brought him along this road **as** Constable McCleary led him toward town.

*

CHAPTER EIGHT

*

"ON YOUR FEET, Mulligan," said McCleary as he led Hans into the pub.

The stools and tables were unoccupied. The day's business hadn't yet begun.

Mulligan put down his newspaper and drew two pints of ale for Hans and the Constable.

"Do you think I could have something to eat?" Hans asked.

"Of course you can. Mulligan, have you got any of your sandwiches?"

Mulligan slid a plateful along the bar. McCleary asked,

"You know who my friend here is? A South African on a walking tour. What do you think of that?"

Mulligan grunted what he thought of it.

"He's walking the entire length of Ireland. And in weather such as this. Strange ways these foreigners have. Of course," McCleary continued, "there's always the possibility that he's not a South African on a walking tour at all. He could be one of the Jerry spies. Why don't you drink your ale?" he asked Hans.

Hans took a sip, and turned toward the policeman. "Is there a men's room here I could use?"

"Why of course there is. Right over there."

Hans got to his feet.

"Well go on man. The ale can wait."

"Aren't you coming with me?"

"What the hell for?" McCleary asked.

"I thought that as your prisoner . . ."

"Don't be daft, man, this is no movie. Did you ever hear the likes of that, Mulligan. He thinks we Irish don't allow a man a bit of privacy."

Mulligan grunted.

Hans hurried off, taking his suitcase with him.

"Is there a window in that room?" McCleary asked.

"Aye, there is," Mulligan replied.

"Big enough for a man to crawl through?"

"Aye."

McCleary reflected upon this bit of information for a moment.

"It wouldn't be locked now, would it?"

"Never is," said Mulligan. "The latch is broken and has been for years."

"Can I use your phone, Mulligan?"

McCleary leaned in close to the wall instrument.

"Connect me with Joseph Donovan," he whispered as he looked out the window and watched a man clutching a suitcase hurrying down the road. "Joseph, it's Seamus McCleary. Our man's on the road to Dublin this very minute . . . Of course I'm sure it's him. Who else but a German would say 'sir' to a policeman? No, I didn't have a chance to tell him anything. You see, I couldn't resist playing around with him a bit, and I'm afraid I frightened him. Tell the lads along the way to keep an eye out for him . . . And listen, Joseph. When you turn in your report to the Organization, don't be giving me credit. It won't do me any good in my profession if you do. I must think of my pension, y'know."

As soon as McCleary was gone, Mulligan grabbed the telephone. "Agnes? Get me Dublin in a hurry. Connect me with Lieutenant Higgens at the Office of the Secret Police."

✳

After his daring escape from the men's room, Hans headed out of town. After two hours of trudging, he stopped in a secluded spot off the road to get his bearings. According to his calculations, he should be close to the town of Gorey, where he'd be able to pick up a train. He'd have to be cautious. The police of Gorey were probably on the lookout for him. He thought of that policeman who was so intent on hanging him, and then had carelessly let him escape. Typical of the Irish, he mused, allowing himself a small smile of victory.

It was dark by the time he saw the lights of the town. He knew he couldn't just walk into the railroad station and buy a ticket for Dublin. He'd have to wait until

63

everyone was asleep. He found a small grove of trees and waited there. A couple of sausages, some stale bread and a few gulps of brandy helped him pass the time.

At ten o'clock he decided it was safe enough to enter the town. The narrow streets were deserted as he made his way to the wooden shack which served as the railroad station. He crouched behind a large baggage cart and waited until he heard the train whistle. He watched from his hiding place as the long line of cars snaked its way past the station. It wasn't going to stop. Hans waited, muscles tensed, until the last car approached. Then he gathered his strength and swung himself aboard.

He crept into the darkened car and found an empty compartment. In no time at all he fell into a deep sleep. He dreamed of climbing through a narrow window with a parachute strapped to his back.

He might have continued dreaming like this right into Dublin Station. But something woke him up. What was it? The train had stopped. He raised the blind and looked out.

Far ahead he saw a platform, and in the background, a sleeping village. Muffled voices drifted in through the glass. Directly below his window were two men. He pressed his ear against the icy window pane to hear what they were saying.

"And it was durin' me supper that I got the word he was last seen over in Kilmuckridge," said the station master.

"Did ye now?" the engineer replied.

"Aye, I did. And I was further informed that he was probably footin' it up to Dublin. But I've me grave doubts about that. It's certain I am that it's on your very train he's ridin'."

"And what is it makes you so certain, if I may inquire?"

"Because no one has seen hide nor hair of the man since late yesterday afternoon."

Hans shivered as he crouched by the window.

An argument followed which was resolved by the engineer. Catching spies was for the police. Not underpaid railroad employees.

But they would telegraph ahead to Dublin and have the police there check the train.

Hans waited until the train started up. Then hugging his case to his chest, he closed his eyes and flung himself to the ground. Over and over he rolled until he came to rest in a narrow ditch.

He lay there until the sound of the train disappeared in the distance. Then he looked about him with anxious eyes. A short distance back was the sleeping town. He'd have to walk to Dublin.

The morning sun found him walking down a dusty road. He was, according to his figuring, about forty miles from Dublin. He sat down to rest, and got to his feet in time to see a car coming toward him. He leaped into its path and waved his arms. The car swerved to avoid hitting him, and sped on. Then he heard the sharp squeal of brakes and he saw the car back up.

"Are you going to Dublin, friend?" Hans called out.

"That we are, friend! Hop in and we'll take you there," replied Chris Kinsella.

CHAPTER NINE

A FRECKLED SETTER studied Hans as he got into the car. She sniffed his barn-smelling clothes and then laid her velvet head on his lap.

"This is most kind of you," Hans told his hosts, as he tried to get comfortable amidst the hunting rifles, boots, picnic basket and dog. His head began to spin with weariness. But he had to think. He had to go over his story. These men, no doubt, were wondering what he was doing walking through the countryside. It shouldn't be a problem, he thought. It's a logical story. But the Irish are such curious people. Better get it over with.

"I'm a South African on a walking tour," he announced. "I'm afraid I chose a rather bad time of year."

Chris and Peadar agreed, and then introduced themselves and gave Hans a thermos of hot coffee.

These men were indeed kind, he thought. Not everyone would pick up a stranger as they did without asking any questions. Such trusting men. The sort he hoped to lead.

He told them more about his business in Ireland. About his study of medieval crosses and slabs—the slab at Innishkea, the pillar at Reask, the Donegal Cross, the North Cross at Ahenny. He saw that they were impressed. He felt more secure and assured himself that whatever suspicions they might have harbored were now laid to rest. His instinct told him that a good spy always covers his tracks. It failed to tell him that a good spy never offers any unasked-for information.

He was exhausted and wished only to sleep for a while.

"When do we arrive?" he asked.

"Oh, by nightfall surely."

"By nightfall?" From his calculations, they shouldn't be more than an hour's drive away. He asked how far they were from Dublin, and Chris and Peadar began to argue whether they were thirty-five or forty-five miles away.

"It was thirty-five when we stopped back there for petrol." said Peadar. "By now it must be closer to forty-five."

A cold chill penetrated Hans, replacing the warm feeling of security he had enjoyed a few short moments before, as he realized that according to this information carelessly offered him, they were traveling away from Dublin, not to it. "Why should it take until nightfall? We're only forty-five miles away."

"Because it's against the law to go hunting within the city limits," said Chris.

He should have been prepared for this. He knew the Irish. They were inefficient, lazy. But no one had told him they were insane as well. Were they all insane, or just these two? Should he get out of the car? He never should have accepted the ride. He berated himself for this un-German weakness.

Peadar helped a little by adding, "We plan to do a bit of hunting first, but don't worry, we'll get you back to Dublin in time for supper."

"Cheer up," Chris said. "A bit of diversion never hurt anyone. And you'll enjoy seeing the Wicklow Mountains on a day as lovely as this one."

What could Hans do but accept the situation? It was better than walking. Besides he was tired. He'd close his eyes and relax.

"You'll have the devil's own time tryin' to get to sleep all crowded in back there," Chris added. "Why don't we change places. There's more leg room up front."

The car slowed and the exchange was made. Hans relaxed and closed his eyes. Suddenly they snapped open.

His suitcase! His suitcase was in the back seat. He couldn't ask for it. He'd arouse suspicion. He'd have to take a chance. After all, it was locked. His brow furrowed into deep lines. Or was it? He couldn't remember. But he was tired. He couldn't keep awake. Yet he must not fall asleep. He said these words over and over to himself.

In a moment Hans Pflug was fast asleep.

*

It was hard for Chris to get comfortable. He rested his feet on the suitcase. He thought about the sleeping South African scholar. Why was he in this part of the country, when the ancient pillars and crosses were in another part?

And his expensive leather case. Most walkers carried knapsacks.

Curiosity was one of Chris Kinsella's minor vices. A major one was the satisfying of it. Should he? It wasn't exactly the proper thing to do to one's guest. What right had he, nosy lout that he was, to inspect a man's private property? None. Having come to this conclusion, he bent down and opened the case.

It wasn't so much the bundle of English pound notes that staggered him, as it was the maps he uncovered. Sufferin' Saints, my maps! The maps he'd traced from an old atlas, re-locating military bases, hospitals and ports in beautiful confusion, then sent to Bridie.

It could mean only one thing. This man asleep in their car was the spy all Dublin was talking about. Holy leapin' Christ . . .

"How's your Gaelic?" Chris whispered. "Still recall any of it?"

"Of course. Why?"

In rapid-fire Gaelic Chris revealed his discovery.

Peadar let out a long whistle. "What are we going to do with him?"

They thought in silence.

Chris decided, "We'll keep him, lad."

"And why not? He's ours, isn't he?" said Peadar as he swung the car around and headed for Dublin.

✳

On the road a plan was hatched. Dangerous, to be sure, but the best Chris and Peadar could do on such short notice.

There they were with a German spy on their hands, placed there by the saints themselves. If they delivered

70

him to the police, there'd be reprisals from the Organization. If they turned him over to the Organization, they'd make heroes of people like Bridie and Duffy, the ones they were out to destroy.

And, of course, there was his money. The police would just impound it. The Organization would use it to blow up mailboxes. There was just one thing to do. Keep him.

They would pretend to be men of the Organization. Chris would be Duffy.

✳

They reached Dublin in time to see the sun shining on the River Liffey.

Hans awoke, expecting it to be evening.

"We changed our minds," Chris explained. "You seemed so anxious to get to Dublin."

And what was more, Hans was invited to stay at Peadar's house, until he found a place of his own.

The idea was appealing. After all, he'd have to make himself more presentable before meeting his contacts. Besides, how could he refuse. In Ireland such things are taken seriously.

He followed his hosts down a narrow alley to the basement room that was to become his temporary headquarters. It had to be the basement, Peadar explained, since his mother was a recluse who wouldn't look kindly on a stranger in the house. He left Chris in charge, and went upstairs for some bedclothes and food.

Hans sank into a tattered armchair. The nap had refreshed him. But his nerves were still on edge. He felt Chris's eyes on him. Before long Peadar came back with tea and sandwiches. Hans liked these men. How friendly and considerate they were. How cooperative. He wondered if he might take them into his confidence. He decided against it. Suddenly it was becoming very hard for him to concentrate. He looked at his friends. Their faces seemed to drift away from him. His eyes closed.

"What the hell happened to him?" Chris asked.

"I just lashed his tea with mother's sleeping potion."

"What in hell for, might I ask?"

"I figured we'd be needing time to talk."

"Neatly figured," said Chris. "But I'm thinkin' we'll need the help of some fellow conspirators. Call Caitlin. And Neil and Johnny, too. Tell 'em there's a game to be played."

CHAPTER TEN

⁜

A BLINDING WHITE light forced Hans to open his eyes. It was coming from a lamp that was turned on him. Beyond it loomed five people in the shadows.

Chris sat behind a desk, leaning on the opened suitcase.

A woman sat on the desk with her legs crossed.

Peadar stared at him from an easy chair.

A tall, heavy-set man stood at the doorway, one hand plunged ominously in his coat pocket.

The fourth man sat beneath the window, his chair tipped back. A cigarette dangled from the corner of his almost lipless mouth. The column of smoke made his eyes narrow into tight slits. His eyes bore into Hans.

Hans saw that it was night. That disturbed him. He couldn't even recall falling asleep.

Who were these men?

Not the police. This was no police station.

Who else then?

Men of the IRA.

But if they were, why this approach? Surely they were expecting him.

Of course! They were being cautious. How were they to be sure of *his* identity? His eyes fell on his open suitcase. What else did they need? He'd play it their way for a while.

"Give me a glass of water," he demanded.

All eyes watched him as he drank.

Neil, a former member of the IRA, had informed them that Standard Operating Procedure in cases like this was for a password to be exchanged. They had decided that the only solution was to bluff the German into giving it first.

Frightening him seemed as good a way as any. And that was why the five of them stood around the room in attitudes that looked like a scene from an American gangster film. Keeping a vision of Humphrey Bogart in his mind, Chris went into action. Regretting that he lacked a wide-brimmed hat to shove menacingly off his forehead with a thumb, he concentrated instead on his cigarettes. He removed one from its package with his lips. Rolled it over to the corner of his mouth with the tip of his tongue, and removed a wooden match from his pocket. From half-drooped lids his eyes burned into Hans.

Casually he scraped his thumb across the head of the match. It snapped in two. He took out another and tried

again. The fourth match finally worked. He lit the cigarette, eyelids drooping even more in the thick cloud of
smoke. Using thumb and all four fingers he withdrew the
cigarette from between taut lips, and leaned toward his
victim.

"All right," he sneered. "Out with it."

"Out with what?"

Chris's upper lip curled. "Identify yourself, pal."

Hans decided to take the offensive. He rose to his feet.
"You know who I am," he said, pointing to his open suitcase. "Now you tell me who you are."

Chris's laugh was a hoarse cackle. "Not so fast. We
know who you're supposed to be, alright. But there's always the possibility you're a fake."

"A fake what?"

"Ah, he's a crafty one, isn't he?" Chris asked over his
shoulder.

"That he is," Peadar agreed.

"The worst sort," added Caitlin.

Hans was beginning to feel battered. "See here," he
said. "Too much valuable time is being wasted by all this.
I am Captain Hans Ernst Pflug, Abwehr II Intelligence
Section of the German Army. Sent here on special duty to
make contact with your organization."

Silence.

Hans was in command. "And now if you'll be good
enough to give me the password, we can get down to business."

Here it was. Chris's brain lunged about desperately.
"Think he's tellin' the truth?" he asked the others. Stall for
time. What German is a match for an Irishman with his
wits about him?

"Hard to tell." Peadar picked it up. "He could be an
Englishman."

75

"Passin' himself off as a spy to gain our confidence," said Neil.

"What we call a 'Double Agent'," added Johnny.

"Right."

Hans felt his assurance slipping. "I'm not a spy. I'm a Liaison Officer."

"Ah. He's not a spy, he's sayin'. That's interestin'."

"And what exactly is the difference, one from the other?" Caitlin asked.

"All I know on the subject is that they hang spies," Chris said. "Maybe they shoot Liaison Officers."

Hans was in trouble. He had to end this silly game. "All right then," he said stiffly. "If you doubt me, turn me in to the police. If not, give me the proper password and end this nonsense."

It was a challenge. A goddamned chess game, Chris thought. And it's I who've been placed in check. His eye fell upon Hans's open suitcase. It focused on the book on top.

"Ulysses!"

"What?"

Chris took a deep breath. It had to be. Why else was he carrying the book? "The password's 'Ulysses'," he said firmly.

Hans was stunned. What was the meaning of the wrong password? Was it possible they weren't of the IRA? Had he made a fatal blunder? A new thought teased him. While it was wrong, it *was* the book to be used as his code control. Was it a test? He couldn't be sure. He decided to go along with whatever it was they were doing. "Yes. That is the password."

It was Chris's turn to be stunned. Back in check. It wasn't possible that he'd hit on the password like this.

What was the German's game in admitting that he had? He had to make his move.

"That's not the password, pal," he said through clenched teeth. "And you damn well know it isn't. So Mr. South African posing as a German, if you don't give us the real one it's a corpse ye'll be." Checkmate, he thought.

The others moved from their positions, and formed a tight circle about the two antagonists. Hans stared at the eyes pinning him to the wall.

How did it happen? Why was he in a position of having to give the password first? It should be the other way around. This nonsense must be stopped. But he'd do it with dignity. He pushed through the circle.

"The password is 'Danny Boy'," he said. "And I must say that I've had enough of this foolishness," he barked. "If we're going to work together in the future, you must realize here and now that things must be done my way." His nerves were jumping. But he kept his face sternly impassive.

"The man's legitimate," Chris announced. "Turn on the lights. Your contact was to be a man called Denis Duffy. That's me. Duffy's me code name. The real one's Chris." He introduced the others and hands were pumped in conspiratorial greeting.

Hans grabbed the reins of command. He strode up and down the room. It would be more impressive, he thought, if he were in uniform. He cleared his throat and peered at the men before him. "In the coming months we shall be working together in a common cause. We shall become as one hand . . . one fist . . . one brain, geared to the ultimate purpose of unifying your country. We shall have important tasks to perform, perhaps even dangerous ones, and I know that you are anxious to hear what they are to be. However, all I can reveal to you at this time is a generalization of our aims. Later, when things are better organized than this and I've met with your superiors, we can go into the specifics. Now I will put before you the things that must be done before we go ahead with the planned operation.

"Firstly, I insist on more comfortable quarters. It's impossible for me to operate from space as confining as this. Secondly, I will need a new uniform to replace the one I was forced to bury on the beach. I must be protected by the Geneva Convention should I fall into the hands of the enemy. Thirdly, I will need a wireless with which to contact my superiors in Hamburg. This is most important.

"And now I wish to congratulate you in the name of my Government for the glorious and daring raid on the magazine fort which you and your valiant men engineered. It was masterly."

Staggerin' Christ, Chris exclaimed to himself, it's getting better and better. The four men and Caitlin stared in amazement at this German strutting up and down.

"Well," Chris drawled, "points one and two can be taken care of easily. But point three might give us a bit of trouble."

"Why?" Hans asked.

Chris frowned. What *was* point three? Caitlin stepped in, "Because wirelesses are illegal now, and it'll take a bit of doin' to get our hands on one. It'll take a bit of bribery I'm afraid."

"Then do it," Hans ordered.

"It'll cost," Chris said tersely.

"I beg your pardon?"

"Money."

"Oh, of course." Hans took the bundle of pound notes, and peeled off five.

"Since you're wantin' it in such a hurry," Neil said, "we'll need at least twice this much. Many's the hand that'll require greasin' ye can be sure." Hans counted out five more.

"About those other matters," Chris said, "they'll be taken care of immediately. You just stay right here and think up all the things you want us to do to unify our country. And we'll do 'em, won't we lads?"

"That we will."

"Righto."

"You can bet that bundle of fivers."

More and more Hans was getting to like these men. "We're about to change the course of history, comrades."

*

Upstairs in Peadar's room they gazed at each other. They had never seen anyone like this Captain Pflug, strutting about, slapping his thighs as though on a Prussian parade ground. And the extraordinary fact that German Intelligence seemed to know nothing of the failure of the raid.

"I guess they just don't get the late editions over in Berlin," gloated Neil.

"As long as they get English pounds, we'll never complain," Peadar added.

"Your scheme's a grand one, I'm admittin'," Johnny said. "And there's no doubt in me mind that it offers up some delightful prospects. But . . ."

"But what?"

"Well what do ye mean by sayin' ye were goin' to buy

79

a wireless for the German. Ye well know I've more than a few of me own."

"Of course I do. And it was from yourself I was plannin' to do the buyin'."

"But why do ye have to bribe me?"

"Because the money's been allotted for that purpose of course. So how much do ye want for one?"

Johnny thought. "Well, seein's as none of them have a radius of more than a couple of miles, how about two pounds and a bottle of Jameson's?"

"You're a hard man," Chris laughed. "It's a deal."

"Now it's a celebration at Neary's that's in order now," Chris said.

"What about the curious people wonderin' about our new affluence?" Johnny asked.

"You recall that uncle of mine, don't you," Chris said. "The one who never existed and never went off to America to make a fortune as a police chief or Mayor?"

"Aye, that we do."

"Well the poor old soul just passed on and left me all the money he never made."

CHAPTER ELEVEN

THE SPY WAS missing. Throughout Dublin questions were being asked, heads shaken. There was no doubt that he'd arrived. He'd been seen by both police and IRA informers. Both groups assumed he'd show up at Murphy's. But he didn't.

Inspector Gallagher concluded that the Organization themselves had the spy. The Organization decided the police had him.

Confusion reigned as Hans slept his second peaceful night in Peadar's basement. It was less peaceful upstairs, where his associates were pondering over a sheet of paper covered with numbers—Hans's message to be sent by wireless to his colonel. The longer they stared, the less sense the code made. So they dumped the problem into the lap of Johnny Nolan. Anyone who could make head or tail of his complicated collection of tubes, condensers, transformers, and also tap on a little key to make contact with other clever lunatics, should be able to crack a code.

So Johnny alone had to achieve the impossible. If the messages were not decoded, they couldn't put together an answer to send back. And if the Captain didn't receive an answer, ugly suspicions would arise.

The numbers stared back at him. He read them backward, forward, vertically, horizontally. No sense at all. Hours passed. He stared, he worked. But the numbers remained meaningless. His books said that if the code were based on some book used as a control, it would not only be necessary for him to know just what book that was, but what page and line of the book was used to form the code. That was impossible. He tried mathematical approaches. These were endless.

Again and again he tried. Each approach ended in failure. Failure meant the end of the game.

Dawn found him still at work, a pile of crumpled papers high about his legs. Was he or wasn't he a mathematical genius? Sure he was. He even had prizes to prove it. Well, here was his chance to add another prize to his list.

When Chris and Peadar returned with coffee and sandwiches they found Johnny asleep with his head on the desk.

"Is it done?" they demanded as they shook him awake.

"Of course it's done," he muttered.

"Did ye hear that, Peadar? Our genius here has cracked the blasted code."

Johnny held out a sheet of paper. But something was wrong.

"What happened?" Chris asked.

"I cracked the bloody thing, all right. I made the numbers into proper letters. But the letters don't make sense. Not the littlest bit of blasted sense. The German has outsmarted us. He used a code within a code."

"It's lost we are," Chris said. "Lost and outsmarted."

He handed the sheet of paper to Peadar, who looked, then smiled. "Johnny me lad, you may be a mathematical genius, but you're sure as hell not a linguistic one. Your code within a code is not that at all. It's German!"

Chris looked at the paper again. "Of course it's German. Why in bleedin' hell shouldn't it be? The man's German, isn't he? And he's sendin' his messages to Germany, isn't he? So why should he send it in English just to make it easy for us?"

*

The reply to his message was delivered to Hans along with his lunch. He opened his copy of *Ulysses* to the previously agreed-upon page, located the appropriate line and word, and set to work. In much less time than it took Johnny, Hans decoded:

GOOD WORK—PROCEED AS DIRECTED—FORWARD. VON F.

That was a puzzling reply. Surely more praise was due than those impersonal words. What did the Colonel mean by "FORWARD"? Did it give him more authority to plan on his own? That must be it. He was on his way. He'd have to start planning immediately.

✻

✻

CHAPTER TWELVE

✻

IN THE PRE-DAWN mist of Dublin, a black
police car moved through the deserted streets. The two
men inside were silent. One kept checking his wristwatch.
At a nod from the time-keeper, the driver threw the engine into high gear. The car leaped forward and rounded
a corner into Merrion Square, where the two policemen
were to deliver top secret documents to the British Legation.

When they got out of their car, another car, with head-
lights extinguished, screeched around the same corner.
The driver got out, pistol in hand. Without a word spoken

by any of the men, the policemen raised their hands above their heads. The gunman took the documents and returned to his car. When the car was out of sight, the policemen fired their revolvers into the air. Then they jumped back into the police car and followed the other one.

✳

At Park Gate, the telephone rang. "Right-o," said Gallagher. "We're leaving now. Tell the boys to get rolling according to plan. Inform the Press."

He hung up and turned to his associate, Higgens. "The incident's taken place. Got the list?"

Higgens nodded.

"Good. Stay with me." Gallagher placed his battered hat on his head and strode from the room, Higgens close at his heels.

They crossed the courtyard to the waiting car as four others filled with men sped out ahead of them, tires screeching.

That morning, officers of the law knocked on doors. Behind those doors lived Dubliners whose lives were furtive, perhaps outlaw. The doors inched open. Search warrants were displayed and greeted with hard faces and harder eyes. The police moved through each house, checking rooms, closets, attics, basements. The occupants in no way hid the fury they felt at this intrusion. Such things were not new to these people and their families before them. Yet since the days of the Trouble less fear attended them. But the anger remained.

Their fruitless searching over, the police left. And the people ran to their telephones to ask in hushed tones if similar raids had taken place in other homes.

The failure of the search was reported to Gallagher. Not a single member of the IRA or any sympathizer was harboring the German spy. Not a room, closet, attic or basement yielded any clue. The Organization did not have the spy. "Goddammit," he swore. "If they don't have him, and we don't have him, then who in blasted hell does?"

※

The communication was marked "urgent." But then everything lately was marked "urgent," Dr. Poetsch thought, as he read:

URGENT: PERSONAL TO AMBASSADOR
HAVE RECEIVED NO WORD FROM AGENT DANNYBOY SINCE
ARRIVAL. HAVE YOU INFORMATION TO WHEREABOUTS?
HAS HE BEEN ARRESTED? FIND OUT WHAT YOU CAN AND
REPORT BACK AT ONCE.

> COL. VON FALKENHORST
> ABWEHR II   HAMBURG

"Gott im Himmel," he moaned. This was too much. If that Hamburg colonel insisted on bothering him, he'd have to send a message once and for all that would stop this nonsense. He'd tell him that as far as he knew there was no German agent in Ireland. And even if there was, he didn't want to have anything to do with him. Goddamn that von Whats-his-name, he thought. Why doesn't he find something else to do instead of torturing me?

※

Herbert Gallagher studied Poetsch's answer that had just been monitored. He had thought that maybe the spy was working through his Ambassador. This spy was not only a challenge to his professional standing, but to his curiosity as well.

"Holy Mother Mary," he muttered. "Was there a spy after all?"

CHAPTER THIRTEEN

THE SPY WAS, in fact, huddled in the back seat of a car. In the front were two very frightened men. Chris and Peadar. Their city seemed fraught with danger. A police car going in the opposite direction made their hearts pound. A shrill voice almost made them abandon the car.

They were transporting a wanted German spy across the city. Transporting him to a large country estate. The owner was a German who considered his Swiss Chateau safer than his Irish one. He turned the latter over to Neil's real-estate office. There wasn't any chance of it being rented, and it was too far away from any neighbors to arouse suspicion.

The tense silence of the three men was broken only when the car entered the grounds of their hideaway through the iron gate in the high stone wall.

"We made it," Peadar said.

"Of course we made it, you faithless heathen," Chris replied. "There was never a doubt that we would."

"Come along, Captain," he said to Hans who was still huddled in the back seat. "Here's your new headquarters."

The three men piled out of the car and hurried up to the thick oak door. Chris knocked three times. It swung open and they disappeared inside.

It was an ancient house. The walls were lined with darkly-painted portraits of ancestors and musty tapestries. Hans was satisfied. It was perfect. Best of all were the grounds—acres of tree-planted earth enclosed behind a high stone wall. Just right for the maneuvers he had planned. It was true that some of his future plans were not included in the briefing his Colonel had given him. But Hans had convinced himself that the word "Forward" with which von Falkenhorst had closed his message to him could only mean that he was to use his initiative in furthering their operation. During the long hours he spent in Peadar's basement, he decided that once he'd accomplished the things he was told to, he would go ahead on his own and organize a raid on the docks of Belfast. A raid that would cripple that life-line to Britain. This was, he felt, an operation worthy of him.

"Very good, gentlemen," he announced. "You are to be congratulated. No more suitable place could have been found for what I have in mind."

Chris tried to match his tone to the German's. "And what exactly do you have in mind, Captain?" he asked.

"To use this house and the grounds surrounding it to train the assault group."

"The what?" shouted Chris, Peadar and Neil.

"The assault group. The men you are going to supply for the raid on the shipping facilities in Ulster."

"Oh," Chris said. "Of course, the raid on the shippin' facilities in Ulster. D'ye hear that, lads? There's goin' to be a raid on the shippin' facilities in Ulster."

"Yes," Hans went on. "This lull in the fighting will not last forever. And when it's stepped up, we will want the English to have as much trouble on the home front as possible. This is where you and I will come in. To harass them in every way we can. And in so doing we not only help Germany but further the cause of a united Ireland as well."

How powerful his voice sounded. This was the beginning. "I am here to guide you and organize the fight for you. This is our golden opportunity. We must use it."

From the rapt expressions around him, he was certain he'd made an impression. These were good men. There was no nonsense about them. No unnecessary questions. They recognized a leader. How German, he thought proudly. With these men he could envisage only a successful conclusion to his glorious mission.

"The raid on the Ulster docks is number one on our schedule," he went on. "We must train the men. We must conserve our ammunition. There will be no more mailboxes blown up."

"Right," said Chris. "Hear that lads? No more blowin' up of mailboxes."

"Right," echoed Neil and Peadar.

"After the successful immobilization of the docks, we can plan another raid to secure more ammunition," continued Hans.

"An excellent idea, Captain," Chris agreed. "We'll use the same men to do it."

"Good. And now gentlemen, let us remember that England's adversity is Ireland's opportunity. We must manufacture that adversity." Hans consulted his notebook, and began to itemize what he would need. First on the list was his uniform. He pictured himself directing the maneuvers in full field uniform complete with binoculars and swagger stick like von Falkenhorst's. He also ordered a dozen lorries with petrol and drivers to go with them. They would have to be large enough to transport the assault group across the border to Ulster. They would have to be equipped with small arms, grenades and anti-personnel mines, and about fifty men. He would need also a few dozen toy soldiers so he could plan his assault in miniature.

Chris, Peadar and Neil watched this performance in amazement. They stared at the voluble little captain as he strode about the room like a field marshal. When Hans paused for breath, Chris mentioned a problem. All those lorries would cost a lot of money. They were even harder to come by than radios.

"About seven or eight hundred pounds would do it," Chris said.

"More like a thousand, including the petrol," Peadar contradicted.

"Right," said Captain Pflug. "Now when can we have the men?"

"When do you need them?" Chris asked.

"As soon as possible."

"Why so quickly?"

"To drive the lorries, you clod," Peadar told him.

"Why do we need fifty men to drive twelve lorries?" Neil wanted to know.

"No, no," Hans interrupted. "We only need twelve men to drive the lorries. The other thirty-eight are for the assault on the docks."

"You mean the other twenty-eight," Chris said.

"What?" Hans looked at him blankly. "Excuse me, but fifty minus twelve is thirty-eight."

"Ah, so it is," Chris agreed. "Sorry." He turned to Peadar. "Make a note to round up fifty men for the assault."

Hans decided it was time for him to send a message to his Colonel. What he needed now was a cadre of German paratroopers to help him train the Irishmen. He clicked his heels and went off to his task.

The three conspirators stared at one another. It was too much to toss at them all at once. They tried to assure themselves that after a good night's sleep they would figure out some way to placate this over-ambitious spy.

Suddenly Chris came to life. "Sufferin' Saints, that lunatic's gone upstairs to prepare a message to Germany."

"Where the hell's Johnny?" Peadar asked. "He's got to receive and answer his goddamned message."

"Follow me lads," Neil said.

The three men walked down a long hall. They came to another broad stairway leading to the second landing. There they came to a small circular stair, steep and narrow and made of wrought iron.

"Where the hell are ye takin' us?" muttered Chris.

"You'll see." They followed Neil up the twisted stairway. At the top was a door. Neil pushed it open. "Behold," he announced.

"Welcome," said Johnny Nolan, "to Abwehr II wireless receiving center, Hamburg."

✳

An hour later, Johnny received Hans's request for troops. He had barely finished his second cup of coffee when the clicking of the message resounded throughout the small room. He leaped to his post and began taking down the coded string of numbers. He squared his shoulders and reached for the books on codes and ciphers and the German-English dictionary.

The dim sunlight sneaked in through the high oblong window. The numbers became letters. The letters changed. Re-changed. And soon there was a message.

Johnny studied Hans's request for trained paratroops. He reached for a fresh sheet of paper and drafted the reply:

IMPOSSIBLE RELEASE PARATROOPS YOUR USE. KEEP UP GOOD WORK.

Johnny was proud of his answer. He thought of the history books of the future that would credit John Nolan with keeping German soldiers from dropping out of the sky on Ireland.

CHAPTER FOURTEEN

※

JOHNNY DROVE HIS uncle's two-ton lorry through Dublin's suburban streets with abandon. Neil and Caitlin, who were with him, clutched each other in fear at each unexpected swing.

"Take it easy, for the love of Christ," Neil pleaded. "You'll cause the death of us all."

"Don't worry, lad, I'm in complete control of the bloody monster," Johnny replied, as he took the next bend in the road without slowing down. "Use the brake, you lunatic," shouted Neil.

"Which one is that?" Johnny asked gleefully.

"Oh, my God," moaned Caitlin.

Neil stretched his leg across the seat and tried to push down on the brake. His foot entangled itself with Johnny's. The accelerator was depressed even further. The lorry careened up the soft shoulder of the road, its engine groaning. Then it stalled. Neil pulled Johnny over his own lap and Caitlin's and took over.

Johnny fumed. It was his lorry. Hadn't he borrowed it from his Uncle Mick, and without even telling him? If it was discovered missing, who would get in trouble?

"We're here," Neil announced. "The front entrance is around the corner. We're ten minutes early, but we better start so Johnny can get the lorry back."

"Be ready to make the change," he said as the others got out. And the lorry lurched forward. Caitlin and Johnny watched. The taillights vanished. They waited. The sound of the engine faded, disappeared, and then was heard once more.

"Here he comes," Caitlin whispered. "Get ready."

The roar of the engine rushed toward them. Caitlin unhooked the chains that held up the tailgate. Johnny untied the rolled-up tarpaulin, letting it fall full length.

"Do the other side too," Neil ordered.

"What for?" Johnny asked. "He can't see the other side."

"Do it anyway, you clod."

Johnny got the other rope untied. The lorry leaped forward. The second round began. The lorry re-appeared. Caitlin announced that the run was made in exactly three minutes forty-two seconds. Neil kept the engine racing. Caitlin hooked up the tailgate. Johnny lifted the tarpaulin to half-mast and gave Neil a bright plaid hunting hat. The lorry started up.

The over-worked lorry careened around the high stonewalled enclosure. It slowed down in front of the gate so Captain Pflug could see more than a mere blur drive by. Again and again, Neil rode this strange merry-go-round.

"I need a rest," he gasped. "I'm dizzy."

Johnny jumped in and the lorry took off in a cloud of dust to break Neil's round-trip record by a full minute. It roared past the waiting pair without stopping. Back again, and this time Neil was ready. He leaped aboard. Caitlin saw it disappear around the corner with Neil clinging to the running board. When it came back, Neil was behind the wheel.

"You crazy lunatic," Caitlin screamed at Johnny. "What are you trying to do, ruin the entire thing?"

"It ran away with me."

A moment later the lorry was once more on its run past the castle.

Round and round, in its gallant attempt to multiply itself twelvefold. Silently and industriously Caitlin and Johnny had done their valiant best to help it achieve that effect. Neil did his bit by changing hats, removing his coat and then putting it back on.

At last, with brakes squealing and engine roaring, the lorry shuddered to a halt.

"Thank God it's over," Neil said. "Now let's get out of here before Uncle Mick has the police on our tails."

"But we only made eleven trips," Johnny protested.

"I make it out to be twelve," Neil said. "What about you, Caitlin?"

"I'm not sure. I lost count."

"It's twelve," Neil said.

"Eleven."

"Twelve, goddamn it. Now let's get the hell out of here."

"Eleven," Johnny said as they drove back to Dublin.

*

"Eleven," Hans said. "There were only eleven. You paid for twelve, didn't you?"

"Aye, but didn't you notice that last lorry, Captain?" Chris said.

"Of course I did."

"Then didn't you notice that it was bigger than the others?"

"Bigger?" Hans consulted his notes, as Chris explained how one three-ton lorry was better than two two-tonners.

Captain Pflug made his official entry in his notebook. There would be ten two-ton lorries and one three-ton for the assault on Belfast. He wrote himself a reminder to replace drivers seven, eight and nine.

He felt good. Action at last.

CHAPTER FIFTEEN

✳

"THIS IS NOT being taken with proper seriousness," stormed Hans.

He turned to Johnny Nolan. "What is going on down there? They are not following my battle plans." He pointed to his private battleground on the table. "I expressly ordered Lieutenant Kinsella to set up an attacking force and a defending force with simulated docks. But all I see out there is . . . chaos! Get out on the field and tell him that I want the maneuvers to proceed *according to plan.*"

Hans studied his toy troops. Those men outside were

not in the least like the ones on his table. He looked out again, in time to see Neil set a camera on its tripod and peer through it. He saw Chris shouting orders through a megaphone, though no one paid any attention.

Even Chris was concerned. But this plan of his seemed the only way out. They had hired fifty of Dublin's actors on the pretext of shooting a film on National Defense. And here was Chris running around as director, and Neil lugging a filmless camera around the grounds. There were so many unforeseen problems—like the bottles his actors brought along with them.

Chris managed to shout them down long enough to explain the seriousness of making a film so Ireland could study how best to repel a possible invader. But then an argument broke out on who the invader was, England or Germany. There was pandemonium as the anti-English and anti-Germans of the group fought it out. The maneuvers seemed to be growing into the real thing.

When order was once more restored, the force was divided into two groups, the Attackers and the Defenders. The Defenders were to be deployed at the site of the "Belfast Docks," a hastily-built structure made up of old pieces of lumber, packing cases, bricks and cardboard. The "Docks" were a short distance from a line of closely planted trees. The trees were the concrete walls surrounding the docks. Whether or not such walls existed didn't interest Hans. He felt they were good for tactical purposes.

On the near side of the trees the boys had dug a shallow trench representing the sea. Chris had objected since the attack was to be made from land. But he was overruled by Hans.

The twenty-five Defenders trudged over the trench, through the trees, and took up their positions on the

"Docks." The attacking force waited for Chris's signal. When it came, hell broke loose. The Attackers, with their wooden rifles over their heads, flung themselves into the water that wasn't in the shallow trench, and waded across to the other side. They were to attack from the trees, and they began to climb. To get a better view, Chris climbed a tree himself. He saw his defending force lying about drinking, card-playing, napping. A rumble of complaint rose from the Attackers.

"Look at 'em, will ye? Enjoyin' themselves whilst we sit up here like a pack of bleedin' apes."

"Makin' like Pashas, inhalin' all that oil while we risk our lives for the National Defense, by Christ."

"What are we waitin' for?"

"Attack!" Chris screamed.

A rain of attackers fell on the defenders with yells, threats and counter-threats. Grabbing for bottles was the rule. The docks trembled under the weight of both fighting units. One end collapsed. From the depths of the broken planks came arms as if reaching from the sea for life-lines. Shouts, curses and a rising cloud of dust filled the air.

"Keep it up, men!" Chris shouted. "You're doin' great!"

Then one weary man lost the battle for all. Bringing to bear his full dramatic talent, he clutched his stomach in a display of mortal pain and fell quivering to the ground. There he took a bottle from his pocket and took a soul-satisfying drink.

His fellow actors stopped. They gazed upon their fallen comrade. Cries of anguish filled the air as forty-nine men died in style. The "Belfast Docks" were littered with corpses.

"On your feet!" Chris shouted. "On your feet, ye louts! This is treason! It's a Government film we're makin', and it's open to charges of treason ye'll be! So on yer feet I'm orderin' ye!"

A new approach was needed. "All right then," he announced. "There'll be ten shillings extra and his name on the screen for every man who's on his feet by the time I count three."

He hadn't underestimated his men. Fifty anxious-to-please raiders were in an upright position by the count of two.

"That's more like it," Chris said. "Now we're goin' to have ourselves another go at it beginnin' from the beginnin'."

Shouts of protest rose. A general revolt was imminent. Chris held up his hand and told the men they could switch groups so that the ones who'd climbed the trees before wouldn't have to again. The fifty men took up their positions.

✳

Hans surveyed the scene beneath him. What had happened to his plans? Why had his docks collapsed? What had happened to his Elite Corps of IRA fighters? What were the strange cries he heard? He saw they were ready to try again.

This was terrible. His maneuvers mustn't fail. How inglorious it would be if they were to be undermined by a group of unmanageable, undependable Irishmen. Anna was right. The Irish are a thoroughly untrustworthy people. But they needed a commander. And he would act like one.

He looked out the window and saw Johnny reading a manual on short-wave radio operations. This peaceful unconcern to the confused disorder around him irritated

Hans more than anything else. "Private Nolan!" he barked. "Take a message to Lieutenant Kinsella. Tell him we're three hours behind schedule. Tell him that this time I want it done right. I want those docks blown up."

Captain Pflug lowered his binoculars and turned from the chaos outside to the ordered battlefield upon the table. He should have taken personal command of the maneuvers, and not allowed Chris to influence him with talk of precautions for his safety. He should have insisted that the maneuvers be held as they would be in the Fatherland.

*

En route to the front lines, Johnny stumbled over the sleeping body of Peadar. He shook him, "Where's Chris?"

"Somewhere out there with his men," Peadar said, rubbing his eyes. "Why?"

"I got a message from his Nibs. He wants the docks blown up."

"So blow 'em up," Peadar said as he turned over to continue his nap.

"He didn't tell *me* to do it. He told me to tell Chris to tell *them* to."

"So tell him for Christ's sake. And leave me alone."

"But I can't find him."

Peadar raised himself on one elbow. "That's the trouble with you, Johnny, you've no initiative. When a good soldier cannot locate his superior officer, he acts on his own."

"You . . . you mean I should blow 'em up?"

"You'll be a hero if you do."

Johnny went to the pile of smoke bombs they'd gotten. When he arrived at the battlefield, he saw the Belfast Docks give way under the furious assault of its former defenders. Initiative was initiative, he thought, as he tied three bombs to a fuse. . . .

*

From his post, Hans stared at the rising cloud of black smoke. He dove under the table.

Chris watched his fifty men scatter in all directions. He did the only thing a good film director could do.

"Lunch!" he called out.

The cheers of the actors brought Hans from under his battlefield table. He witnessed his fifty grimy, smoke-blackened soldiers in the process of settling down on the grass to eat their box lunches.

They deserve it, he thought. It isn't every day that the Belfast Docks are blown up.

CHAPTER SIXTEEN

✳

THE DAY BEGAN wrong for Hans. First there was that disturbing reply from Abwehr to his report on the successful outcome of the maneuvers. He'd expected more than the usual "well done, keep up the good work." And he didn't expect von Falkenhorst's order to discontinue daily messages. That puzzled him. But, he reasoned, Abwehr knew what it was doing. He, of course, had no way of knowing that Abwehr was tired of being cooped up in his tower prison decoding numbers, and was now enjoying a post-maneuver celebration at Dublin's most exclusive restaurant along with Chris, Caitlin, Peadar and Neil.

Toward dusk Hans heard a car stop in front of the house. Chris and Peadar were due back from their meeting with the IRA executive council. He looked out the window, but instead of Peadar's battered car he saw a long black one with two uniformed constables getting out.

What did this mean? Had the boys been arrested? He knew what he had to do. As the constables pounded on the door, Hans burned his notebook in the fireplace, donned his uniform, hid his wireless, and took his military papers from his suitcase. He was safe. If he were arrested, it would be as an officer in the German Army with all the protection of the Geneva Convention. He opened the door to announce his name, rank and serial number.

"Aren't you Heinrich Krueger?" one of the constables asked.

What sort of game was this? Who was this Krueger? He shook his head.

"You're not? Then who are you?"

Was it possible that they weren't looking for him after all?

The constable explained that they were making a routine check of foreign nationals. This house was listed in the name of Heinrich Krueger. Hans wished that his uniform would disintegrate. His brain spun as the constable asked if Hans were not this Krueger, would he inform them where they could locate the man.

Were they deliberately trying to confuse him, Hans's mind raced as he explained he had never heard of Mr. Krueger, that he had leased the house from a private party who had since left Ireland.

He casually raised his hand to wipe the perspiration from his brow, but instead slid his army cap from his head. Then, as though shivering from the cold, he crossed his arms over his chest to cover his insignia.

"Shame you can't help us, mister," the constable said. "And since you can't, I guess we'd best be gettin' on our way."

They were going. He couldn't believe his luck. Such dolts. They were so concerned with their Mr. Krueger that they failed to notice his uniform or how he'd introduced himself.

"Well then, good evening to you, gentlemen."

"Good evening? Why, you're coming with us, Captain. I'm thinking that in Dublin they'd be more than interested to discuss that German uniform you're tryin' to hide."

Herbert Gallagher drummed his fingertips on his desk as he listened to the constable laconically describe the night's routine. The constable was enjoying his moment of glory. It wasn't every day that a suburban constable outsmarted the Secret Police.

"You see, sir," he constable was saying. "The man who opened the door not only wasn't Krueger, but he was someone not on the list at all."

"And that confused you enough to interrupt my dinner."

"It wasn't only that, sir. It was also the way he was dressed."

"I see," Gallagher replied. "It was the way he was dressed. And how, may I ask, was he dressed?"

"Like he was goin' to a fancy dress ball," said the constable.

"Very observant of you, Constable. And because the man was playing dress-up, you decided to call on me."

"Yes sir," grinned the constable. "Because he was wearing the uniform of a German officer. I figured he might be the spy you fellows have been looking for these past weeks."

Gallagher leaped to his feet. "Where is he?"

"Right outside your office, sir."

There indeed was Hans Ernst Pflug, resplendent in his uniform, standing at attention.

It was over at last. The weeks of waiting and searching. The object of the hunt was before him. "Sit down, Captain."

Hans refused. He would behave as von Falkenhorst had ordered him to. He would give no information. He would incriminate neither himself nor his Irish colleagues.

"All right, Captain, I've got a few questions I'd like answered before we get down to the official inquiry with the Army present."

Hans told him that the only question he was obliged to answer was the one relating to his name, rank and serial number. He insisted that he be treated as an honorable political detainee under the rules of the Geneva Convention. He wanted his Ambassador notified. He felt he had carried that off very well. His Colonel would be proud.

"That's a lot of insisting for a man in your position, Captain." Gallagher studied the silent man before him. One of those stiff-necked Army types. The sort that never relaxes.

"Do you suppose that the Geneva Convention could ease up slightly to allow you to tell me where you've been these past weeks, and just why you're wearing your uniform as though you were on a parade ground?"

He was pleased to see the German relax a little. He didn't know it was because his question told Hans that Chris and the others hadn't been caught.

"I refuse to answer the first of your questions. As for

the second, it should be obvious to you that I'm in uniform in order to prevent being executed as a spy. Under the terms of the Geneva Convention . . ."

"I know, lad, I know," Gallagher interrupted. "And a bright idea it was too. Except that it's applicable only in Ulster. Eire isn't involved in the war as a belligerent. It makes no difference how you're dressed."

Hans felt his legs buckle. He accepted Gallagher's offer of a chair.

"Now then, you can make things a good deal easier on yourself if you'll tell me why you came to this country, whom you were to meet, and where you've been these past few weeks."

No answer. The two men stared at each other over the desk. What sort of man was this, Gallagher wondered. He looked ordinary enough. But despite his mistake about the uniform, he was most likely a top agent. He'd been on the loose in Ireland for almost two months with neither hide nor hair of him seen since the first day. And not a clue to his whereabouts during all that time. What in blazing hell had he been up to?

Was it possible that this man had a group outside the IRA? One even more efficient and underground? He'd have to find out about it. From the looks of things it wouldn't be easy. No doubt his opponent was a man of intelligence and dedication. He felt good about that. Learning about him and his activities would be even more of a challenge than finding him in the first place.

"Don't worry, Captain, you'll be treated like a proper political detainee. And you'll probably find life a good deal more peaceful where you're going than where you've been. No more fears of being executed as a spy, are there?"

∗

∗

CHAPTER SEVENTEEN

∗

GALLAGHER HAD IT all figured out. Captain
Pflug was undoubtedly one of the shrewdest agents ever
sent to Ireland—even if he hadn't realized he was in a
neutral country. Gallagher figured this out after the German Ambassador denied knowing anything about Pflug.
This could only mean that not only was he one of their
men, but one of their most important. The Ambassador
must have gotten word to Hamburg that their spy had
been captured. And Hamburg, not wanting the Irish to
know the importance of the man they held, told the Ambassador to deny him. That way the Irish Police would

think that "Danny Boy" was still free and operating in Ireland, and that Pflug was too unimportant to question closely.

Having figured out exactly what German Intelligence was up to, Gallagher went ahead interrogating Hans. He was getting nowhere. Polite, but uncooperative, Hans offered no information whatsoever.

＊

"Check," said Captain Pflug.

It was the seventh afternoon of their tournament. Gallagher sighed. These defeats were demoralizing. Instead of facts, all he was getting were chess lessons. He lit a cigarette and held out the package.

"Thank you," Hans said. "I don't smoke."

"Very clever of you. I wish I could give it up. Did you stop recently?"

"I never smoked at all," Hans said.

"That's strange," Gallagher said. "I'm wondering who filled all those ashtrays we found at the castle."

Not the slightest flicker of a muscle was visible on Hans's face. Let him play his little games, he thought. Let him come and play chess with me every day if he pleases, twice a day even. He'll get nothing out of me. Absolutely nothing. He made his move.

＊

"By the expression on your face I can tell you lost again," Higgens said.

His chief sat down heavily. "He's a very clever man. And a determined one. I'm sure he knows we're on to him, but he's not going to tell us a thing. I'd give a month's pay to know what he's up to."

"How do you know he's up to anything, now that he's out of business?"

"Oh, he's not out of business. I'm certain of that. The warden tells me he's been filling up the notebook I gave him. He spends most of his evenings writing—and throws nothing away."

"Well, why don't you just walk into his room and take it away from him? He's our prisoner, isn't he?"

"There you go again, Sean," Gallagher admonished. "Don't you understand that I can't do it that way? It's guile that's called for, not force. And if you're interested, I'll tell you my plan."

"You've got an idea!"

"That I have," Gallagher replied. "Come along."

"Where to?"

"To the hospital."

"The hospital? Who's sick?"

"Captain Pflug!"

✻

The situation was becoming intolerable. Hans saw himself as a tiger in a zoo. Or an eagle in the cage of a canary. He cracked his knuckles as he paced the floor. He missed his command. He could picture that night he stood with his two lieutenants and watched the parade of trucks. What will happen to them now? Who would organize the attack on Belfast? Only a short time had passed since the day of the maneuvers. Now there was nothing.

He did take pleasure in the fine job he was doing handling that secret service man who played such a bad game of chess. He kept their conversations to such topics as ancient Celtic art. He was proud too that he was able to keep up the model prisoner façade without cooperating. He was counting on this façade to relax his captors' vigilance. For Hans had a plan. A master plan for escape.

His nights were spent filling up his notebook with a design for getting out of Arbor Hill. He was working against time. He had to get back to his men. His plan was a careful one. He even drew maps and sketches. He threw nothing away. He knew how prisoners' wastebaskets were examined by the police.

And he was careful never to let the notebook out of his sight.

He took it with him when he was taken to the hospital for a medical examination. He went along willingly and even enjoyed the ride through Dublin. And at the hospital, when he was told to undress, he took his notebook out of his jacket to put it into the pocket of the robe he'd been given. He made a most odd discovery. The robe had no pockets. Was it possible the Irish wore pocketless bathrobes? Surely all civilized countries possessed bathrobes so equipped. Why not this one?

Whatever the reason, he was forced to leave his notebook behind. But he'd do it cleverly. Instead of attaching importance to his papers by trying to hide them, he would place the notebook in a very obvious position. He put it in his jacket letting some of it protrude. And he measured the portion which protruded.

✻

When Hans left the dressing room, Gallagher and Higgens entered. In a minute Gallagher noticed the notebook protruding from the jacket. He measured the visible portion and then snatched the book.

"You have to think of everything in our business," he commented. "Even removing pockets."

114

They hurried from the room. A police technician awaited them. The pages were separated, and the long work of making photo-copies was begun.

Hans, in the meantime, was having his examination. His doctor put in a call to Gallagher.

"Listen Herbert, I don't know exactly what you're up to, but there's nothing wrong with this man. Can I return him now?"

"How much longer?" Gallagher asked the technician.

"A half hour at least."

"Not yet," Gallagher said. "Think of something else to do to him."

"I thought of sending him to the psychiatrist, but he's off duty."

"Have you X-rayed him?"

"No I haven't. What should I X-ray?"

"All of him." Gallagher hung up. A half an hour later the doctor called again.

"He's turning blue with the cold. And any more radiation and he'll begin to glow in the dark."

"That'll put an end to his spying, won't it?" Gallagher hung up.

Fifteen minutes later the notebook had been replaced, and the two policemen were on their way to Park Gate with the copies.

Indeed it was a daring plan. The two men saw the meticulously executed diagrams of Hans's room and the entire south wing of the prison. His notes showed that he had discovered a hollow space between the ceiling and the roof of the building. His soundings had indicated it was big enough for a man of his build to crawl through. He had found out that the space extended the entire length of the south wing, and that the ceiling was so poorly constructed that with the use of a hammer and chisel a hole could be made large enough for him to enter. According to the notebook, Hans already had these tools. Every step of the escape was outlined, including the spot where he would break through the roof and drop safely into the garden of a private house that adjoined the prison.

"The man's a proper genius," declared Higgens. "We've got to move him out of there right away."

"I have a better idea," said Gallagher.

✻

"Captain," the warden said next afternoon, "I've been giving some thought to your accommodations here. We haven't done right by a man of your position."

Hans looked up from his reading as the warden continued. "Ireland unfortunately isn't properly equipped for the detention of officers of your rank."

Hans studied the man, and wished he could find one Irishman who would say what he had to say instead of making useless conversation.

"What's wrong with where I am?" he asked

"There's not much wrong with it, considering it's a prison cell. But it's not in proper condition for a man like yourself. The window leaks when it rains, the ceiling is spotted in places, the paint is faded and the sink is chipped. How's the mattress?"

"A little lumpy."

"Then we'll get you a new one. And if you won't mind staying in one of the smaller cells for the next day or so, our lads will go to work on this one and get it all ship-shape for you."

How ungrateful it would be to repay the warden's solicitude with an escape. But what could he do? "I won't

116

mind at all," he said. "And I want to thank you for the consideration you're showing me. When I return to Germany I shall be certain to report the excellent treatment I received."

"That's very considerate of you, Captain."

❋

On the first night of his return to his old room, Hans was determined to escape. He turned out his lights early, curled up under his blankets fully clothed, and waited. The prison routine over, the guards dozed at their posts as the long night loomed ahead. A little past midnight, Hans prepared himself. He cut a piece off his woolen blanket and wrapped it around the hammer. He slid the table over to the center of the room and placed a chair on it. He stood quietly in the darkness. One slip and all would be over.

He climbed onto the table and then onto the chair. He removed his instruments from his pocket and, with a grim smile, struck the first blow.

❋

The guard who brought the breakfast tray also carried a broom and dustpan under his arm. Without a word, he swept up the debris of broken plaster and powdery white dust. Not once did he look up to the ceiling nor at Hans who sat on the edge of the bed. His face was pale and he paid no attention to his breakfast.

When the guard finished his work, he turned to Hans. "Dreadful work these plasterers do nowadays."

Hans just stared up at the shiny steel plating that showed through the hole in the ceiling.

CHAPTER EIGHTEEN

*

THE MORNING PAPERS announced the spy's transfer to the escape-proof Mountjoy Prison. Newsboys along O'Connell Street hawked their wares in that unintelligible jargon of newsboys the world over, and people stopped, looked and bought.

Ambassador Poetsch studied the headlines and smiled with relief. His nemesis was at last locked safely away. He prayed the man would stop asking the police to notify him of his ridiculous desires. He hoped that he had the good sense to have supplied himself with a cyanide capsule. What good foresight on his part to have denied the spy's existence to that Inspector Gallagher. And how fortunate he had not notified that annoying Colonel whatshis-name in Hamburg of his spy's capture. Now that the fool was locked up, perhaps the messages would cease. He folded the paper to the comic section and sat down to a hearty breakfast.

*

Herbert Gallagher had no need to read the headlines as he sipped his coffee. He knew the Captain was on his way to Mountjoy. He had ordered the move. His pleasure would have been complete, except that Captain Pflug, although chastened by the failure of his escape, was not defeated enough to start talking. Gallagher began to have doubts about the man. Had he guessed wrong? Was he so important after all? Perhaps he really had nothing to say. Or was he so dedicated that he would remain silent in the face of anything? Gallagher sighed.

*

Chris and Caitlin sat across from one another in a small restaurant facing the quays. The headlines stared up at them.

"What if he talks?" Caitlin asked.

Chris was sure that Hans would never give them away. As long as he felt there was a chance they could still blow up his blasted Belfast docks. "Besides, he's a Secret Agent. Those blokes take cyanide before they talk! It's their code."

Bridie O'Meara shook the black headlines under Beryl's nose. "It's given me ideas," she said. "Lots of 'em. And I've been toyin' with 'em all morning. There's a fine possibility we can do something about gettin' our spy out of Mountjoy. And we'll do it without the bumbling assistance of the likes of Denis Duffy, Murphy or that lamebrained Charlie Kearney—men who cannot plan a decent raid or find a spy who's out searchin' for them."

"Are you saying, Mum, that we should try to get the German out by ourselves?"

"That's exactly what I'm sayin', girl. And not *try* to get him out. We're goin' to do it."

"You have a plan?"

"Indeed I have, daughter. Indeed I have."

*

The O'Connell Street newsboys were gone, having sold out their papers. The Ambassador was tearing up another desperate message from Hamburg. Inspector Gallagher was winding up a routine day. Chris and Caitlin were strolling through St. Stephen's Green. And Bridie O'Meara was initiating the first of a series of moves that would hurl Hans from his comfortable cot in Mountjoy and wrap the tentacles of the game once again about his unsuspecting neck.

CHAPTER NINETEEN

A SLIP OF paper stuck to the bottom of Hans's coffee cup told him to report sick. No signature, no further information. Just to report sick. Chris. Reaching out through the vast network of the Organization, Chris had arranged for his escape.

A half hour later he was escorted to the prison infirmary. Dr. Liam Sullivan, inmate and infirmary physician, preceded him wordlessly into the examining room. He wrote down Hans's description of a vague abdominal pain. A cursory examination was followed by a bottle of brown pills. "Take one of these with each meal, and come back in two days. I'll write you a pass."

No sly wink of conspiracy. No whispered word of encouragement. Nothing except a few squeezes at his midsection and a bottle of pills he knew he didn't need. Had the note been a joke? Or some plan of that wily Gallagher to trap him?

As he started for the door, the doctor fell into step beside him. "Be ready for an escape in two days. And shave close that morning."

Before Hans could react to these words, they were in the outer room in the presence of his guard. "I want you back here in two days," the doctor was saying loudly. "That liver of yours doesn't look too good to me."

In a moment Hans was escorted back to his room with a bottle of pills and a medical pass in his hands, and excitement in his heart.

Two days later was visitors' day at Mountjoy. A clean-shaven Hans sat debating whether he was supposed to go to the infirmary again, or wait for some sign. The sign came in the shape of a guard he'd never seen before. He was told that it was time for his appointment with the doctor. They walked down a lengthy corridor which was not the one leading to the infirmary.

"We're goin' to pass a lavatory in a second. Duck in and change into the clothes ye'll find in the last cubicle. Leave your own there. Don't come out 'til ye hear me knock on the door. The visitors will be leavin' along this corridor. Join 'em and walk out as calm as ye please. Ye'll be contacted on the outside. Ye've got ten minutes."

A few steps more and they came to a door marked "Lavatory." The guard opened the door and shoved Hans through. Inside Hans dashed to the last cubicle. His eyes fell on a pile of feminine clothing. No time to question. He must do as told. Only ten minutes. He stripped off his prison garb down to the skin, and started to re-dress. Beryl's girdle was an instrument of torture. He almost pulled a back muscle trying to attach the black stockings to the slippery little appendages that hung from the girdle. Then he donned the brassiere, and frowned as it hung emptily from his shoulders. He added his socks and undershirt to one cup and his shorts to the other. They now bulged appropriately—but unequally. At least they bulged. He pulled Bridie's black dress over his head. The high neck was tight, but it fit better than the girdle. He then turned to a large purse that lay partially open. It contained a wig, a kerchief and make-up. "I can't," he thought. But he must. He went to the mirror and applied eyebrow pencil, lipstick and a circle of rouge on each cheek. He toned it down some with great shakes of the powder puff. He inspected the results in the mirror. Obscene was the word that came to his mind.

He'd never pass as a woman. It was ridiculous. Yet it was his only chance. He put on the wig, and tied the black scarf under his chin. "Obscene," he muttered, and donned a woolen coat.

Then he put on the shoes. High-heeled shoes that were too tight. He stood up shakily as perspiration gathered under the thick layer of face powder. A loud knock sounded. One final look in the mirror and he stumbled out into the corridor to join the line of home-going visitors.

"Move along, Mum, you're holdin' up the line," the guard said.

Hans found a place in the line of women, most of whom were dressed in black as he was. He noticed that a few of them hid their faces in their handkerchiefs as they sobbed for their loved ones left behind. Hans took a handkerchief from the purse he was carrying, and sobbed pitifully into it. Shuffling, teetering and staggering, he sobbed. He sobbed down the long corridor and he sobbed past the outer gate. The guard didn't have the heart to bother him for his pass. He sobbed halfway down the cement walk before he realized he was out.

He was free. He looked about him at the cottages that lined the walk, wondering if anyone inside was noticing his peculiar gait or make-up. He straightened his wig and tried to adjust his hips. How easy it was. How incredibly easy.

He breathed deeply as the sounds and smells of freedom swirled about him. Then a hand gripped his arm and he almost fainted with fright.

"Come along, Auntie, or we'll never get home in time for tea." He turned to face Beryl O'Meara.

She guided him toward Drumcondra Road. To all appearances, they seemed to be two women clinging to one another in common grief at leaving a beloved in Mountjoy. This was certainly not an uncommon sight on this street.

"It's not far now," Beryl whispered.

Then the prison sirens sounded. Hans almost fell. "Pay no attention." They walked as rapidly as they could to the tune of the wailing sirens. They reached Derrymane Parade where there were two women's bicycles waiting. "Can you ride?" Beryl asked.

"Yes," Hans answered. But his spirits dropped at not seeing Peadar at the wheel of his car. "Who are you?" he demanded.

"My name's Beryl O'Meara, and I'm from the Organization. Now climb on this bicycle and follow me."

O'Meara, he thought, as he mounted the bicycle. A familiar name. Caitlin O'Meara, Chris's girl friend. Wasn't he told that she was of a good IRA family? This no doubt was her sister. He felt better. It was many years since he'd been on a bicycle, and it took a few minutes before he could control it.

The rise and fall of the sirens was joined by the higher-pitched wail of police cars. Hans felt his heart rise up into his throat. Beryl remained stubbornly unconcerned.

As they approached Drumcondra Bridge, they were stopped at a roadblock.

"Well now, ladies," the sentry demanded. "Where are ye goin' in such a hurry, if I may be so bold to inquire?"

Beryl's bright smile and flashing eyes had their desired effect on the young man. "We're gettin' away as fast as we can from the unearthly noise emanatin' from those toys your pals are playin' with. It's bringin' on me poor Auntie's migraine somethin' awful, so it is."

"Aye, they're a noisy lot to be sure," he agreed. "But it cannot be helped Miss, with an escape so recently per-pertrated from Mountjoy."

"I'm sure you boys are only doin' your duty, and it's a good and lucky thing for poor Ireland that ye are. Now would ye mind please, if me Aunt and me pass through, she's fair perishin' for want of her tea."

The sentry looked at her aunt in time to see a fallen stocking being hooked on to a garter with a few inches of bare thigh momentarily visible.

"Go along then," he grinned at Beryl. "And if it's back in this neighborhood ye'll ever find yourself, I can be located at Harry's every afternoon at four."

"Can ye now?" Beryl replied coyly. "Well, if ever I am in this neighborhood, I'll be certain to drop in."

CHAPTER TWENTY

※

HANS CLIMBED STIFFLY from the bicycle and stumbled into the O'Meara house. He collapsed on the couch and tore off his shoes. Before his wig was off, Bridie bounded into the room:

"Welcome to the house of the O'Mearas!"

"Mum," Beryl interrupted. "The police know he's gone. They'll be lookin' all over town for him. We've got to hide him at once."

"Right ye are, daughter. Into the secret room with him." She stopped herself halfway to the trapdoor. "No, that's the first place they'll look." And as she stood there thinking, a police siren pierced the air.

"Quick," Bridie said. "Go out through the kitchen door, hop over the back fence and go into the house opposite. Tell Mrs. Brady you're on the run from the police. She'll know what to do."

"But can the woman be trusted?" Hans asked.

"When it's runnin' from the police ye are," Bridie assured him, "all Ireland can be trusted."

As the police pounded on the front door, Hans escaped through the rear. And as Bridie opened her door to her uninvited guests, a middle-aged woman opened hers to Hans. She took him to a bedroom where a wooden closet was shoved aside to reveal a small door in the wall. She slid it open and pushed Hans in.

✳

"I tell you, Beryl," Bridie said to her daughter as the two policemen rolled back the rug, "this indignity foisted upon us innocent citizens by forces of so-called law and order is too much to take. Upsettin' the peaceful household of innocent women, burstin' in here without a sign of manners or warrant, to plunder and destroy."

"Now, now Mother, don't go gettin' yourself all flustered. There'll be no plunderin' and destroyin'," the policeman assured her.

"Don't you be callin' me Mother," Bridie fumed. "Your own mother, poor soul, was no doubt the illegitimate daughter of an Englishman."

One of the policemen went down and examined the secret room. Then they rolled back the rug and went upstairs to the bedrooms. After an unsucessful search they returned.

"All right, Mum, if ye'll be so kind as to show us your downstairs rooms, we'll be castin' a quick eye over them and ye'll be seein' us leave your premises."

"It's not your leavin' here that I'm lookin' forward to seein'. It's yourself hangin' from the end of a rope that I'd enjoy feastin' me old eyes upon, ye traitor to Ireland."

She turned to Beryl. "All right now, child. Show this rabble the back room and kitchen so that they can be leavin'. Then we can set about fumigatin'."

As soon as they left, Bridie was on the telephone. Once again the closet was shoved aside, and the small door slid open. Hans was released and led out the back door. As he disappeared over the fence, his hostess opened the door to the two policemen. They went directly to the bedroom, shoved the closet aside and slid open the small door.

*

Two hours later found Hans dressed in the late Mr. O'Meara's Sunday best, and stuffing himself on the sausages, sauerkraut, black bread and beer that Bridie had stored up for his visit. Here he was, the spy all Ireland wanted to get their hands on, sitting at her table.

It was this sight that greeted Caitlin when she came home.

"Captain Pflug," she cried from the doorway. "What are you doing here?"

"Miss O'Meara, how very good to see you again. Where's Chris?"

Caitlin tried to adjust to this weird situation.

"What's the meaning of this, Caitlin?" Bridie roared.

Caitlin was desperate. She had to do something to save the situation. Chris and Peadar were at Neary's carrying on about the trouble they'd be in once Hans told his story to the Organization. But instead he was having dinner at her house.

"Answer me, Caitlin," Bridie was saying. "And what has that Kinsella to do with it?"

She had to say something. So she told the truth, at least as Hans knew it. She and Chris, she explained, had for a long time been part of the highest council in the Organization working under Monaghan himself. Their most important assignment was to work with Captain Pflug. This was a top secret operation.

"I don't believe it," Bridie said.

"Nor do I," exclaimed Beryl. "And I suggest we call Monaghan direct and ask him."

"You can't do that," Caitlin blurted.

"And why can't we? If it's the truth, why should ye fear our callin'?"

Captain Pflug was on his feet. "Madame. I suggest that it would be most unwise for you to make that call. Every word your daughter has said is the truth. You are not to do anything that might jeopardize my mission here. Is that understood?"

Bridie and Beryl could only nod dumbly. Caitlin used their silence to relax and question Hans.

"How did you get out of Mountjoy, Captain?" she asked.

It was Hans's turn to be confused. He was certain she would have known of Chris's part in his escape. But before he could answer her, Bridie unfolded her entire plan and its smooth execution by Beryl and Liam.

Caitlin was playing her role to the hilt. She berated her mother severely for doing something as important as this without consulting the higher-ups. "I hope you haven't ruined things," she said. "What on earth did you plan on doing with him? Hiding him in your secret room where the police would find him?"

Bridie was not quite shattered, for over-riding her disappointment was her pride in this daughter of hers.

"Daughter, I shoulda known it. I shoulda guessed. And if I didn't, it's not that I'm stupid, but because bein' an O'Meara, you're so clever that you outsmarted even me. It's proud I am of ye, Caitlin. And that goes for your Chris as well. Such a fine lad he is. No wonder he stood up to me, for it's of strong stuff he's made. 'Tis a cryin' shame his poor parents aren't alive to see him now."

Caitlin fought back a smile. "I must report to Chris," she said, and ran to the telephone.

"Darling, you'll never guess who's at my house for dinner. . . ."

✳

"One question I must be asking," Peadar said as they raced across town, "and that is just what are we supposed to do with a spy who has no money? For it's more of a liability he is now, you'll admit. To say nothing of harboring an escaped prisoner. That could be sticky."

Chris agreed. But they still had to keep Hans from talking to the Organization. That could be stickier.

"Coming in?" Chris asked as they parked the car.

"Never, I'll wait out here and keep the motor running like a true outlaw."

"Coward."

✳

Bridie watched Chris and Hans greet each other. Chris Kinsella striding about her parlor taking charge of her spy. It was a bitter pill indeed for her to swallow.

133

"Well, Mum, that was a wild operation ye managed. Too bad it was premature."

Mum is it? she thought. But then she looked at the new Chris Kinsella. "I tried me best . . . son. And now, it gives me great pleasure to welcome you as a fellow fighter for Ireland's freedom. In times such as these, portentous with promise of success, it's of infinite importance to have the likes of you on our side. Together we shall all go forward."

✳

Hans was glad to leave, even if it did mean returning to Peadar's basement. For one thing he was worried about the police coming, as Caitlin had warned. And he was anxious to hear Chris's plans.

Bridie had stood by stoically as they left. She had held out her hand to Hans, and was delighted when he kissed it. And she had given him a carton packed with cans of German food. She stood watching as they drove off with her spy.

CHAPTER TWENTY-ONE

THE SPY HAD escaped! Vanished! Throughout Dublin newsboys shrilled the news. Citizens shook their heads. Herbert Gallagher shook his. His man reported that the Organization didn't have him. He was back asking himself if we don't have him, and they don't have him, then who the hell does?

Ambassador Poetsch cursed the spy. He thought of bolting his doors, disconnecting his telephone and wireless.

He might have, too, had he known what the spy was considering.

"I'm reluctant to use this procedure," Hans complained. "I was instructed to stay away from my embassy."

But he had to get back to Germany. And this was the only way. Hans was despondent. From any standpoint he was returning to the Fatherland a failure. He had not gotten his weather station or his U-boat refueling base or his permanent radio contact. And now he had to appeal to his Ambassador like a whipped puppy.

"Perhaps I should stay on a bit longer. There's still so much to accomplish."

"Now, now, Captain," Chris consoled him. "The sites for your bases and stations have been chosen. All we need is the money. Your job is to get to the home office and take care of that."

Hans's silence signified his reluctant agreement. So they devised a plan. A plan to get Hans to his Ambassador to demand a submarine to take him back to Germany. The early hours were best since the police watchers would be asleep. The only problem was the vicious dog that prowled the grounds.

Dogs petrified Hans, especially Dobermans. But this Doberman wouldn't bother him, he was assured by Chris.

Three A.M. found them parked alongside the high stone wall surrounding the German Legation on Northumberland Road. Chris got out of the car and opened the rear door. "O.K. Neil," he said. "Hand 'er over."

Wagging her tail joyfully, Neil's hunting dog, Duchess, licked Chris's face. "Don't be lickin' that traitor," Neil scolded. "He's no friend of yours."

With Peadar's help, Chris and Duchess got to the top of the wall surrounding the German Legation. The dog on the other side growled. Neil shut his eyes as his dog was lowered over. The growling ceased. Chris gave the signal, and Hans was up and over too.

"I should never have agreed," Neil moaned. "Sacrificed to a German. How'll I ever get rid of the pups?"

✳

While the Doberman in the garden was diluting the purity of his race, Hans was at the front door of the Legation. But he couldn't just ring the bell. He'd climb through a window. Once inside, he made his way up the stairway. He entered the first door he came to. He saw a figure curled up on the bed, and touched it gently. The figure sat bolt upright and started to scream. Hans placed his hand over the mouth.

"It's all right," he whispered in German. "I'm the spy who escaped from Mountjoy."

He switched on a lamp, and before him was Lore Poetsch, blonde and lovely in her sheer nightgown. He stood frozen.

"Who are you?" he asked. "Where's the Ambassador?"

Lore smiled and stretched. The blanket fell away. She was not the kind of girl to miss such an opportunity.

"He's sleeping. Can't you tell me about it? I'm his daughter."

Hans took a step back.

"Take one more step and I'll scream," said the resourceful young lady. Hans stood rooted to the spot. He was desperate. He thought of the Doberman outside and begged to be taken to her father.

She got out of bed and inched closer to him.

Her voice was seductive as she described the drama of their situation—an escaped spy on the run from the police finding safety in the bedroom of his Ambassador's daughter. She elaborated on the plight of a lonely German girl in a land of cold Anglo-Saxons.

"And so they meet," she breathed. "Two outcasts from society, who for a tiny moment find fulfillment together. He returns to the Fatherland carrying with him the bittersweet memory of that night. It's like a movie come to life."

Her co-star backed up. "Young lady, you are a bad advertisement for the Fatherland. You should be sent back to work on the land. Hard physical work is what you need. Take me to your father at once."

The spies she'd read about never resisted. What was wrong with this one? He was worse than Scherrf. Maybe there was something wrong with all German men. Too busy fighting and marching about in uniforms. Let them send her back. She'd set things right. There was nothing to do but take him to her father.

Doctor Poetsch fumed with anger at being awakened from a dreamless sleep. He stormed downstairs to his study to find Hans sitting in his favorite chair. "What do you think I am, a spy center?"

Hans leaped to his feet. "I am Captain Hans Ernst Pflug currently on special duty with Abwehr II serving directly under Colonel von Falkenhorst."

"Then what are you doing in my house, disturbing my sleep? Why don't you go about your special duties?"

"But you must have heard of me, Herr Ambassador. I'm Danny Boy."

"Danny Boy is a sentimental Irish song."

What was wrong with this man? Von Falkenhorst had said he could expect no help if he got caught. And no doubt the Ambassador has his instructions to follow. But this was different. He had to get out. He had to make his report to Abwehr and return to complete his mission.

"My dear sir," Dr. Poetsch said, "I have told your cloak-and-dagger colonel that I am not to be included in his games. I will not assist a fugitive from justice. German national or not."

"Herr Ambassador," Hans began. "Must I remind you that the Fatherland is at stake. Our Fuehrer is trying to win a war. Our duty is to help him. I must insist that you contact Germany and arrange for a U-boat to pick me up. It's time you diplomats did some work."

"Herr Pflug," Poetsch said. "You came to this country without my help. You escaped from prison without my help. I suggest you return to Germany without my help."

Hans began to speak but then his eyes fell on something very strange. "Where did you get that bathrobe?" he demanded.

"I beg your pardon?" the Ambassador said.

"I asked where you bought that bathrobe you're wearing. In Ireland or Germany?"

"In Ireland. Why, what's wrong with it?"

"It has pockets."

The thought suddenly came to Dr. Poetsch that this man was mad. He'd have to treat him in a different manner. He could not jeopardize his comfortable position by visits from this lunatic. It would be wiser to take whatever risks were necessary to rid himself of that possibility. The man was obviously mad. Von Falkenhorst wanted to get rid of him so he sent him to Ireland. What a lovely revenge on that interfering, spy-crazy Colonel to send his lunatic back to him.

"What do you want me to do?" he asked.

✳

Three nights later Hans was on his way back to the Fatherland. He was more determined than ever to return. He read for the tenth time the story spread over the front page of the paper Chris gave him before he left. The thrumming of the submarine engines matched the pulsing in his brain as he read of the daring raid that destroyed the Belfast Docks. He thought of what it must have cost them to pull off this brave act.

But Chris didn't mind the cost. Ten pounds and a bottle of Jameson's wasn't that much for a dummy front page.

CHAPTER TWENTY-TWO

*

"YOU BUNGLING FOOL, where the hell have you been?"

"Why, sir, I've been in Ireland."

"Don't be funny," von Falkenhorst snarled. "I didn't think you were on the French Riviera."

"I . . . I don't understand, sir."

"You don't understand? I don't understand. Why haven't I heard from you all these weeks? Not a word, not a single message until your cowardly cry for help to get you out. I should have left you there except I was curious to find out what you were doing instead of what you were sent to do. Well?"

"Well, what, sir?"

"Wellwhatsir, wellwhatsir, is that all you can say? I want to know what you were doing. No wireless station, no weather station, no U-boat refueling base, no liaison with the IRA. Nothing!"

"But I blew up the Belfast Docks."

"Oh, you did, did you? And when may I ask, was that remarkable feat carried out?"

"The day before I left Ireland."

"That's nonsense. On top of everything you're a liar. You must be insane."

Hans brought forth the newspaper Chris had given him. Von Falkenhorst frowned.

"You're still a liar. And considering all your other bungling, I'm inclined to believe it was done by persons unknown as it says."

Hans's mind went blank. He stood there, crumbling slowly into shattered fragments of the hero he'd been. But what of the messages he'd sent? The replies he'd gotten?

Von Falkenhorst was saying he had never gotten any messages from Ireland and had never answered any messages he'd never gotten. He accused Hans of being a double agent in the pay of the British! Of course he could not punish him for being a double-agent when he was never officially a single one. Hans Ernst Pflug, Abwehr Agent, did not really exist. His file from sub-center Nuremberg had been destroyed and the pilot who'd flown him to Ireland had been transferred.

"Get out of here, *Private* Pflug," he whispered hoarsely. "You are relieved of all duties and are to consider yourself under house arrest. Go home and stay there. When

the fighting starts in earnest you'll hear from me. Mean-
while I order you on pain of a firing squad to speak to no
one about this. Do I make myself clear?"

Hans nodded.

His Colonel leaned across the desk. "Now get out of
my sight before I strangle you."

✳

Hans went home to Munden a beaten man. He had no
idea why his Colonel had acted as he had. And how
was he ever to get back to his colleagues in Ireland?

"Eat," Anna said. "It'll do you good. For three days
now you lie here not eating and not talking. It's not
healthy."

"I'm eating, Anna," he protested.

"Not enough. Your father, he was an eater. And he had
energy. You don't because you don't eat."

"I'm not hungry."

"Why aren't you hungry? It's not natural for a young
boy like you not to be hungry. What did they do to you
in Nuremberg?"

"I wasn't in Nuremberg, Anna. I was in Ireland."

"On one of those walking trips of yours. I should have
known it. You've been poisoned by foreign food."

"I wasn't eating foreign food. I was eating kraut and
sausages mostly."

"No wonder you got sick," she exclaimed. "What do
those aborigines know about kraut and sausages. I don't
like the way you look. What happened to your lovely
curly hair? It's getting grey and thin." When did her
Hansie grow up? "Where's your father's picture?"

"In Mountjoy Prison."

143

"What's your father's picture doing in prison? He won't like that. He was never in prison before."

"I left it there."

"That's very careless of you, Hans."

It was too much for him. He had to talk to someone or go mad. It was safe to talk to Anna. She wouldn't understand a thing anyway. "Sit down, Anna, and I'll explain everything. It's rather complicated I'm afraid."

"Good," she said with interest. "I like complicated things. Your father always said I had a good mind for understanding complicated things."

Hans explained the whole thing. And Anna listened with a gleam in her eyes. When she heard of the scene in von Falkenhorst's office, she uttered the two words that immediately put every piece of the puzzle in place for Hans.

"He's lying."

Hans sat upright. "What did you say?"

"I said he's lying. He's jealous of you. He wants all the credit for himself. It's obvious. It's getting to be a common thing among these upstart young officers we have in the army nowadays. If von Hindenburg knew of it, he'd do something, mark my word."

"You know," he said at last, "you could be right."

"Of course I'm right. Your father always used to say, 'Anna is right.' Don't you remember?"

"Yes. Yes, I do, Anna."

"Then why didn't you listen to me when I warned you against going off to foreign lands where heathens poison you with ersatz German food?"

"I'm listening to you now, Anna. Tell me more about what you think."

"Well," she began, "To my mind it's like this. You say that you sent messages in a code that only Abwehr knew, and they were answered in the same code. Yet your colonel tells you he never received your messages. So who answered them if he didn't get them? Obviously he got them. So, he's lying. And he's lying because he's typical of all those big shots who order young men like you to risk their lives for the Fatherland while they stay safely at home to steal the credit."

"Of course," Hans nodded. "How clever of you, Anna." His mind whirled. It was all clear. And he was furious at the injustice of it.

"There's nothing I can do about it, though. If I go to Berlin with my story, von Falkenhorst will deny the entire thing. Even deny that I was in Ireland on his orders. And the Army will listen to him and not to me."

"So don't go to the Army. Go to the SS."

"Why should they listen to me?"

"Because they're not on very good terms with Abwehr, that's why."

Hans was dumfounded. "What did you say?"

"You heard me, Hans. You're not deaf. Why do you make me repeat myself? You know I don't like to repeat myself."

"But Anna, how can you make such a statement?"

"It's easy. I just don't like repeating myself. There, you naughty boy, you made me do it again."

"No, I mean about the SS and Abwehr."

"What about the SS and Abwehr?"

"That they don't get along well."

"Oh, is that so? Feuding are they?"

"But you just said they were," he sighed.

"Then don't make me say it again."

"But . . . but . . . how do you know?"

"Don't stutter, Hans. My nephew told me."

"Your nephew? What nephew?"

"Klauss Ehrhardt. You remember little Klauss. The boy who threw you in the river that time we had a picnic on the Wesser."

"Ah, yes, is he still throwing people in rivers?"

"Don't be silly. He's got more important things to do than that. He's a Colonel in the SS. I'll call him and tell him to visit me. If I bake him some cookies, he'll be sure to come. Then you can tell him your story and he'll help you."

"And Klauss told you about the SS and Abwehr?" Hans asked.

"Of course he did. Who else do you think would come here, eat my cookies and unburden himself? Von Hindenburg?"

Anna was in her element. Her Hansie had given her something to do. She was going to do it like in the old days. She would call little Klauss in Berlin and tell him to come to Munden at once. She'd bake his favorite kuchen. He'd listen to Hans's story.

Hans was unconvinced, and especially since von Falkenhorst warned him not to speak to anyone. He was reluctant to take a chance.

Anna's voice was firm. "Of course you'll take a chance. Doesn't von Hindenburg take chances? It's your duty. You owe it to your country and your Kaiser. You tell everything to Klauss. All about Ireland and your code and your Colonel who's trying to steal your glory. Tell him or I'll be cross with you."

"All right, Anna. I'll talk to him. It's a chance I must take not only for the Fatherland, but for my Irish comrades as well." He felt better.

Anna nodded in approval. "You go to sleep now," she instructed. "I'll leave your window open from the bottom, and tomorrow bright and early I'll call Klauss." She bent over to let Hans kiss her dry wrinkled cheek.

"Anna," he murmured. "You're a marvel."

✳

Hans couldn't sleep. He kept thinking of all the things he'd say to Klauss. He'd tell him how restless the Irish were, how desperately they needed a leader. How he was the logical man for the job.

The twelve lorries became fifty. The fifty men became five hundred, all fully armed and ready. The million rounds of ammunition had another million alongside it in warehouses throughout the country. The weather station and U-boat base needed only the final touches to begin operations.

He would convince Klauss that if he didn't come through, von Falkenhorst and Abwehr would grab all the credit for themselves. And if he did come through, he would tell Klauss, there was for him that castle outside of Dublin.

Yes, he would return. His comrades needed him. Were probably expecting him right now. No doubt they were already waiting for a secret message to bring them the good news. He wouldn't disappoint them!

Hans fell asleep with a smile on his face. With the help of the boy who once tossed him into the Wesser, Hans Ernst Pflug would soon be on his way back to his command.

CHAPTER TWENTY-THREE

"WHAT IN GOD's name is that?" Chris asked, as he and Caitlin approached the corner table.

"Your guess is as good as mine," Peadar replied. "It's for you. It came by Special Post, to you care of Neary's Pub."

Chris placed his ear to the package. At least it wasn't ticking. But he didn't know anyone in Switzerland who would send him a parcel. Nothing to do but open it. He removed layer after layer of brown paper until he came to a white cardboard box. Inside was a two-tiered chocolate cake, surrounded by lacey paper. Tiny flowers of sugar icing framed the words:

HAPPY BIRTHDAY DANNY BOY

"Now what the bloody hell kind of joke is this? It's not me birthday and me name's not Danny. Danny Boy is a . . . Holy Saint Pat, it's from himself. What's he doin' in Switzerland?"

"It's probably poison," Peadar said. "Paying us back for what we did to him."

Chris stabbed into the cake. The blade struck something hard. It was a small metal box. Inside was a piece of paper:

WATCH THE WINDOW IN FRONT OF MY EMBASSY. TWO DAYS FROM THE DAY YOU SEE A FLOWER POT PLACED THERE, I SHALL RETURN TO THE PLACE OF MY DE-PARTURE. MEET ME THERE. I SHALL BE IN DISGUISE. DANNY BOY.

They couldn't believe it. Why should he be coming back? Was it possible that he didn't find out that no messages had been sent or received? Could he be returning to exact some terrible revenge? Then why warn them with the cake? There was only one answer. For some reason he hadn't discovered their trick, and he was indeed returning to continue his mission.

"But why did he bother with the cake at all, and what's this business with the flower pots?" Caitlin asked. "He could have just sent a letter from Switzerland."

"Don't ye see," Chris said. "Whether he knows it or not, he's playin' the Game like a true Irishman!"

*

The German Ambassador to Ireland read the message on his desk. It wasn't fair. His life had been so uncomplicated since he'd gotten rid of that madman with the fetish for bathrobe pockets. The Irish Secret Police had at last finished questioning him about the escape from Mountjoy. And Danny Boy, he hoped, was in the madhouse where he belonged. Or better still, shot. And now he was to place a flower pot in the front window of his legation the following morning to welcome another one of those idiots! Who was this annoying SS Colonel named Ehrhardt, who signed the message? He ought to send a message right back telling him if he wished to play games with flower pots to come over and play them himself.

But an SS colonel was not to be treated with the same disrespect as an Abwehr man. Doctor Poetsch sighed. He'd reply to his new tormentor that his orders would be carried out. He would do what he could without jeopardizing his own position.

*

Herbert Gallagher was bored. Things hadn't been quite the same since the German had disappeared. There was much he would never know about him.

When a copy of the message that went to the German Legation was brought to him, he snatched it. What did it mean? Obviously the flower pot was a signal. But to whom? And why was the SS sending an agent instead of Abwehr?

Whatever it all meant, at least things would be picking up. His spirits soared.

*

Chris Kinsella strolled past the railings of Trinity college on his way to the German Embassy. It was his turn to make the morning round. He enjoyed bright Dublin mornings with young girls swinging their hips above shapely legs. Down Nassau Street into Lower Mount. Perhaps this was the day. The day a flower pot would mark the new start of their game.

He was directly opposite the Embassy. Not a flower pot in sight. But just then a pair of hands placed a pot containing the most beautiful geraniums he'd ever seen on one of the downstairs window sills. His cigarette dropped from his lips as he hurried down the street to a telephone booth, whistling "Danny Boy" through the clear air.

※

※

CHAPTER TWENTY-FOUR

※

THE NIGHT WIND was blowing off Dingle
Bay bringing the salt sea-taste to the lips of the waiting
group. They were back on the same beach where they
had waited for the submarine to take the Captain away.
Now they were waiting for it to bring him back. They
listened to the rhythm of the waves, as they peered out
at the ribbon of moonlight stretching to the invisible
horizon. Chris checked his watch, and faced the four
other members of the welcoming committee waiting on
the beach.

"Are ye sure you're up to it, Mum?" he asked.

"Of course I am. What d'ye take me for?"

I take ye for an old sea cow and not lead oar on the Oxford crew, he retorted silently.

"But Mum," Beryl protested, "it's been years since you've rowed a boat. Better let me do it."

Bridie was disdainful. "Rowing is something one never forgets, like riding a bicycle. Now shove off," she ordered.

While Bridie and Beryl disappeared into the moon-dappled water, the rest of the team took up their posts. Peadar as look-out man went to the top of the hill. Chris and Caitlin waited on the beach, talking of the adventures to come.

"What happens when Mum catches on to all this?" Caitlin asked.

"Why should she catch on?"

"Because you can't keep her running about forever without asking questions. To say nothing of her hearing something from Duffy or Monaghan."

"Don't fret yourself so much," Chris told her. "Your Mother's a true Irishwoman. She'll forgive me. For what else can she do to the father of her future grandchildren?"

Caitlin thought of something else. How would they keep their spy from invading Ulster?

"We have a plan," Chris told her. "One that'll keep our lad so occupied he'll have little time to think up dangerous tasks for us to be carryin' out. Peadar and I have decided that it's high time the Captain got himself some fair lass to dally with. In return for the honeymoon cottage he's provided us, the least we can do for him is to make him over into an Irishman. And since he hadn't the good fortune to be born one, the next best thing is to marry one of those wondrous specimens Ireland produces."

To Chris's way of thinking, the cake and flowerpot incidents proved their captain ripe for conversion. And that his German officiousness was merely an outer skin covering a confused and gullible man. "The Germans are probably using him the same way we are," Chris said. "And for much worse reasons. He's the sort who'll always be used by someone. He's like the cake in 'Alice in Wonderland' with the words, 'eat me' on it. All that Teutonic nonsense has been laid on him too thick. It's our duty to peel it off and show him how life should be lived."

Caitlin insisted Chris's scheme would never work.

Chris was undaunted. "For ye well know," he was saying, "There's not a human being alive who, if he stays long enough in Ireland, won't fall under the spell of Kathleen ni Houlihan."

Caitlin smiled as she heard Ireland referred to in that allegorical way. It was the name left over from the Bad Times when England forbade the use of the name Ireland.

They were interrupted by a far-off, insistent throbbing.

"What's that?" Caitlin asked.

"It isn't a submarine that's makin' a sound like that." Chris looked about. Up on the hill he saw Peadar looking skyward and pointing excitedly.

"Look!" Caitlin cried.

They squinted their eyes upward and saw the outline of an airplane swoop low out of the clouds. In the pale moonlight the plane dipped low and cut its engines.

"It's a plane he's comin' in! Not a sub!"

Chris reached for the binoculars just as a dark shape dropped from the belly of the plane and tumbled earthward. The plane roared into the blackness.

A parachute billowed out above the falling figure.

Down through the night, sillouetted in the light of the low hanging moon, the figure of a black-robed nun swung

155

gently under an umbrella of silk. The white winged cap was caught by the breeze and floated outward like angels' wings. The face beneath it, half hidden by the starched band that framed it, wore a look of determination mingled with joy.

Drifting slowly to earth, skirts billowing and heart pounding, was Captain Hans Ernst Pflug, Irish Expert and Master Spy, returning to the waiting arms of Kathleen ni Houlihan.